Utsuro Bune

The mystery of the
hollow ship

PREFACE

In a time of wonders and mysteries, in the province of Ibaraki on the east coast of Japan, an extraordinary event occurred on February 22, 1803.

As reported in Kyokutei Bakin's 1825 book 'Toen shōsetsu', some fishermen made a discovery that would ignite the imagination and curiosity of generations: an unusual boat stranded on a sandbar just a few feet from shore.

The vessel, completely circular, with a diameter of about 16 feet and a height of 10 feet, had a singular structure: the upper part, made of red wood, contrasted with the lower half, made of an unknown metal. Windows closed with metal planks and enigmatic writing on the hull added to the mystery surrounding this strange ship.

But the real surprise lay behind those windows: a young foreign woman with hair as red as fire, surrounded by such an aura of mystery and charm that those who saw her thought she was a princess. Her presence, accompanied by a bizarre box, aroused awe and fear among the villagers.

At a time of isolation and suspicion toward foreigners, the local community was faced with a difficult choice: report the unknown to the authorities or reject them.

The decision was made: the boat was resupplied with provisions and sent adrift, leaving behind unanswered questions and speculation about the origin and fate of the enigmatic woman and her strange ship.

Thus was born the legend of the Utsuro Bune, the 'Hollow Ship,' a tale shrouded in mystery that continues to enchant and to intrigue the imagination of anyone who approaches its history.

UTSURO BUNE

THE MISTERY OF THE HOLLOW SHIP

ANTONIO MORI

BERGAMO, ITALY

Saturday, January 12, 2019

"Nothing yet", thought Gabriele, moving his chair closer to the monitor with a slight squeak. The cursor blinked as if to challenge him, an impatient opponent waiting for his next move. Around him the world had evaporated: no work emails, no calls, just a Saturday afternoon devoted to his project.

Programming video games was not his main job but a hobby created to fill the evenings when Netflix offered nothing interesting, or the Saturdays when tennis matches did not call him to the court. Sometimes he fantasized that that hobby could turn into a little extra income, just enough to indulge in an extra pizza, but, that afternoon, as he wrestled with a rebel code, that dream seemed light years away.

He was working on a car racing simulator on checkered paper, an idea germinated during boredom hours in high school several years earlier. Now, turning that idea into something playable on a mobile phone had become an almost personal challenge. But there was a problem: he couldn't get multiple players to run on the same track. Every change to the code led to errors, and each time in a different way.

On Gabriele's desk, next to his computer, was a small wooden Zen Garden, complete with a bamboo rake with which lines could be drawn in the fine sand. At that moment, Gabriele felt particularly tense. His hands reached for the rake, gently moving it through the sand.

This ritual not only distracted him but also allowed him to find a moment of peace and regain the focus needed to resume work.

He had traced the first marks in the sand when: *Ding-Ding.*

The familiar sound of a new WhatsApp message interrupted his train of thought. Gabriele lifted his gaze from the laptop screen, one eyebrow raised with curiosity as the notification lit up his cell phone screen.

From Luna: "Hello Gabriele, nani shite iru?"

Luna... Gabriele looked away from the phone screen to look out the window of his room, which looked directly onto the small garden of his ground-floor apartment. It was a peaceful corner he had carefully set up, surrounded by a low wooden fence that added a rustic touch to the surrounding urban environment. A light sprinkling of snow had gently whitened the plants but the raspberry and rosemary bushes were still distinctly visible, offering a pleasant contrast to the white of the fresh snow.

In the center of the garden, the young cherry tree that Gabriele had recently planted stood out with its bare branches, lightly covered with snow. It would still be a long time before its delicate white blossoms, tinged with pink, would bloom again, transporting Gabriele back in memories, to the hanami days he had experienced during the three years he had spent in Japan.

Gabriele lived in Bergamo, a small town in northern Italy located about an hour's drive from Milan. He lived in an apartment block in the center of town, on the ground floor, with his own small garden. With the extra money he earned working as an expatriate in Japan, he had had to make an important choice: get an airplane pilot's license and buy a new car or buy an apartment. His desire for security and aversion to risk had led him to choose the apartment.

He had chosen that arrangement for several reasons. First, it was close to his place of work, a practical factor that saved him valuable time every morning. In addition, it was within walking distance of his mother and sister's house, which allowed him to be close to his family and, not secondary, to have food always available in case of emergency.

The small garden was another aspect that had convinced him, although the only thing he could cultivate was the *dream* of a lush oasis, as his plants always seemed to have other plans. Still, he liked the idea of having his own green space where he could relax and enjoy some peace and quiet. The garden, though simple, had become a corner of peace for Gabriele. He loved spending time there, especially during nice days, perhaps reading a book or simply enjoying the outdoors.

Most importantly, he wanted to live near a cherry tree; he could no longer live without it.

He picked up his cell phone again, looking at the message preview with a mixture of excitement and awe.

Luna had been the most important person during his years in Japan, the person with whom he had shared the most moments, visited the most places, and learned the most. He had not heard from her since the previous September, since he had said goodbye to his friends at their Roppongi gathering, the day before he returned to Italy for good.

"Hello Gabriele, nani shite iru?" The message contained only those words.

During his three years in Japan, Gabriele had studied the language or, at least, tried to. At first with great commitment, excited to immerse himself in the culture and in the language of the Land of the Rising Sun. He often found himself immersed in grammar and vocabulary books, trying to decipher the kanji characters in a similar way to how he would resolute a Sudoku puzzle, but as time went on, his motivation waned, overwhelmed by daily commitments and the frustration of not seeing significant progress. Nonetheless, although he was far from having sufficient knowledge, Luna knew that he would understand at least 'nani shite iru'. "Hi Gabriele, what are you doing?"

So, the literal translation was easy but understanding the significance of the message was quite another matter: they had not heard from each other for five months, the goodbye had been painful for both of them, and now, such a trivial message? Just to resume the conversation? It was Saturday afternoon in Italy, so Saturday night in Japan.

In response, he opted for a light tone.

"Hello Luna, hisashiburi! I'm at home, working on the computer. And you are dancing in Roppongi?"

Gabriele smiled at the mere thought that Luna might spend Saturday nights in Roppongi, Tokyo's nightlife district: the height of Luna's nightlife was bowling or darts; considering how much she loved the study of foreign literature, particularly Italian literature, she was more likely to be at home, wrapped in blankets, reading a book. He had also gone out of his way to use another very common word, one of the first he had learned: 'hisashiburi,' 'it has been a long time'.

Luna's response confirmed his expectations, "Ha! Nice! And I guess when you say you're working on the computer, you're actually working on your own little games." She replied in Italian. Unlike Gabriele's Japanese, Luna's Italian was perfect. Perhaps in speaking she could recognize some imperfection in pronunciation, mainly because of the confusion between the B and V, but otherwise her Italian was impeccable.

"Can I call you for a moment?" wrote Luna soon after. Gabriele's throat went dry, and he snapped to his feet and looked around to sure was no one there, despite only he lived in that apartment.

Whenever Gabriele had to make a phone call, whether it was to order a pizza or to discuss important matters, he felt the overwhelming need to stand up and walk back and forth.

He swallowed, drew a deep breath, clicked on the phone icon on the app and initiated the call.

"Hi Luna, what are you doing up at this hour! Go to sleep!"

"Hi Gabriele! How are you? Long time no talk!"

Well, Luna wanted to keep the conversation light, without talking about 'them'. He would have been vague as well. As in all such cases, he would start with the weather.

"Eh yes, everything is fine. A light snowfall has come, finally, but still not enough to have good ski slopes. On the other hand, it's very cold. How about on your end?"

"No snow here but very cold, in fact Saturday night at home!"

"How come you call me so late?" he asked.

"Gabriele! You don't imagine! I was in Ibaraki yesterday, at the Prefectural Museum of History."

Ibaraki, located on the Pacific coast, was only 100 miles east of Tokyo but, despite its proximity to the metropolis, it remained one of the least developed and populated areas in the region: tourism was limited and business activities scarce.

Traveling by train from Tokyo to Ibaraki required about three hours, a considerable amount of time compared to the nearly 400 miles one could travel westward along the Tokaido line in the same amount of time. This relative isolation had kept Ibaraki sheltered from the intentional urban development that characterized other areas near the capital. However, this had also left Ibaraki in a kind of economic and social limbo, making it less attractive for investment and development and giving it a reputation as a neglected and forgotten area compared to the vibrant dynamism of other Japanese prefectures.

"To Ibaraki? And what did you go all the way there for?"

"There was a conference on the Satake clan, active during the Edo period. The library where I work commissioned me to conduct research on this clan for a conference we plan to hold in the spring. The museum in Ibaraki, given the long history of the Satake as daimyo, the political leaders of the region, has an extensive collection of documents about them. Taking advantage of my visit, I asked Kiyoshi-san if I could explore the museum's archives that are not normally accessible to the public. Do you remember Kiyoshi-san?" He remembered Kiyoshi, he had been Luna's teacher at the university, they had all gone out together a couple of times to play darts in Shibuya, then, a few months before Gabriele returned to Italy, he had moved to... Where? Oh yes, just to Ibaraki. From there he had had no contact with him.

"Of course I remember him. I got against him my greatest achievements as a dart thrower."

"Eh, bravo, you used to play with him every weekend, you even bought your own custom darts, he had never thrown any before. Now he's the director at the museum and he let me go around their archives for couple of hours."

"And did you find anything interesting?"

"I leafed through a binder containing documents on tax collections and financial records from the late 18th century..."

"Wow! What an exciting topic! I can't wait for you to tell me all the details!" exclaimed Gabriele, with a veil of irony.

"Baka!" called Luna a fool to him. "Looking at those documents, we could find a whole world of interesting facts. They might tell us about how taxes were collected and managed but also more human stories of people trying to avoid payment or corrupt officials. Who knows, we might even find records of unusual situations, such as the most outlandish excuses for not paying! In short, there is a lot of intriguing material hidden in those archives that could uncover surprising aspects daily life in Japan's past. However, that's not what I wanted to talk to you about."

"Fortunately!"

"In short: in a binder I found an Italian flag!"

Gabriele was so surprised that he stopped thinking about how boring the subject of finding Luna must be.

"Impossible... In the late 18th century there could be no Italians in Japan... And maybe the Italian flag didn't even exist."

"However, it was definitely an Italian flag," retorts Luna.

"And it couldn't have ended up in the wrong folder, maybe the one from a century later?"

"The flag was in an envelope, accompanied by an inscription in Japanese that said: 'filed in the fourth year of Bunka's reign,' so about 1807. And wait until you hear the rest! There was a very ruined embroidery on the flag, but I was able to read the word 'Lombardy,' or something like that."

'Even more strange' thought Gabriele; Lombardy was the Italian region he was living in.

"Do you have a picture? Will you send it to me?"

"I didn't take pictures, it didn't seem right considering it's a restricted area of the museum, but maybe I'll go back and have another look and ask Kiyoshi-san if I can take some pictures. Then I'll send it to you!"

"Great! So maybe I can find out where it came from." Luna knew that in addition to having some skills in using software, which could help analyze details of the flag that were hardly recognizable to the naked eye, Gabriele also had a strong passion for history. Perhaps in Italy it would have been easier to find information about that flag.

"Very well! I'm going to sleep now, bye!"

"Oyasuminasai!" Good night.

She was always the same Luna, always passionate about any topic involving history or literature... But that flag was really strange, it couldn't have been in Japan in the early 1800s.

Good. Gabriele had feared that the conversation might veer into topics he was not ready to deal with, talk about the last few months in Japan, the decisions made together, the reason for such a long silence. Instead, it remained very friendly and on a decidedly interesting topic.

So, what was that slight sense of nausea he was feeling?

Was he really glad he didn't address the open issues?

His gaze stopped on the painting hanging on the wall, the work of his father. The painting depicted Don Quixote and Sancho Panza in a familiar scene but with a unique twist that had always fascinated him: the hero of Cervantes was charging against a windmill on his tall horse, while Sancho Panza and the other characters laughed at him. However, hidden behind the mill was a terrible monster visible only to Don Quixote from his elevated position. The others, from the ground, saw only the mill and laughed at the hero. The picture offered a reflection on the confrontation between reality and imagination, a conflict that he now felt acutely, comparing the reality of the call he received with the imagination of how it might have unfolded differently. As he had learned to do over the past few months, he staked everything on reality, pushed this thought into some drawer in the back of his brain, and went back to the 'little game' he was working on.

TOKYO, JAPAN

Friday, September 25, 2015

The Yamanote line was like a big hug that wrapped around the heart of Tokyo. It was a loop that connected the most vibrant and central areas of the city, such as Shibuya, Shinjuku, and Ikebukuro, where life never stopped, to the slightly quieter neighborhoods of the very first suburbs. Inside the line was the pulsating soul of Tokyo, with its skyscrapers, stores, and bright lights, while outside we began to see a Tokyo was a bit calmer, residential, but still incredibly close to the action.

Taking advantage of the Yamanote line, from Ebisu, the station closest to where he lived, getting to Tokyo Station was quite easy. Fifteen minutes without change and he would arrive at his destination.

He had moved to Tokyo a little over a month ago, and that was his first social outing: an aperitivo organized by the Italian Chamber of Commerce in Japan, where Italians, mostly expatriates like himself, and Japanese who had some relationship with Italy met.

Gabriele had joined Automitalia, a multi-national Bergamo-based manufacturer of automotive mechanical components, only a few years earlier. Soon, executives had recognized him as the perfect candidate to expand the company's presence in Japan and offered him a move to the Tokyo office for three years. In this position, Gabriele would be tasked with increasing company's presence in the Japanese market and acting as a technical, commercial, and, above all, cultural liaison between Japan and Italy.

The move, for Gabriele, represented not only a professional challenge but also a unique opportunity for personal growth. He had always been fascinated by Japanese culture, its history, art, and philosophy. Living in Japan would give him the chance to fully immerse himself in this culture, learning the language, exploring the social and business dynamics, and making important connections with the Japanese people.

Not having many close ties in Italy, except for his mother and sister, who had made him promise to return often to visit them, Gabriele could accept this opportunity with a relatively light heart.

Preparation for the trip had not been particularly challenging. With little time on his hands and some familiarity with Japan, where he had already been several times for short periods, he knew that he would be in a safe place and that, one way or another, he would get away with it.

There was only one thing that really worried him: food. Gabriele had always been very selective food. He could live comfortably on pasta and pizza for months and, every time he tried something new, he risked an empty stomach.

He clearly recalled one evening during one of his business trips to Japan, when a Japanese colleague had invited him to a renowned sushi restaurant. Sitting at the counter, with the cook preparing the set menu in front of them, Gabriele had faced one of his worst dining experiences, despite the fact that the food was undoubtedly of the highest quality. Rice with a slice of salmon or tuna was manageable, in fact, delicious, but when it had switched to swordfish, he had begun to feel uncomfortable. The climax was reached with the fish pupils: at that point, Gabriele had given up dinner and suffered from nausea for two days. Since then, he vowed to avoid fixed-menu dinners.

For language study, he had started to look at something out of curiosity even before he left Italy, but he gave up quite early. He was completely lost when he discovered that words could sound the same but mean different things depending on how they were written: the sound 'ame' could mean 'rain' if written 雨 or 'candy' if written 飴; 'hashi' 'bridge' 橋 or 'chopsticks' 箸; 'kaeru' 'frog' 蛙 or 'going home' 帰; 'kami' even could mean 'hair' 髪, 'paper' 紙 or 'God' 神...

He had asked his Japanese colleagues how they could distinguish the meaning of these sounds communicated verbally instead of written, and they had replied "from the context." "Okay," Gabriele had retorted, "but if I just say 'kami', how do you understand what I'm talking about?" They replied by shrugging.

In short, he would reconsider once in Japan.

Thus, on August 23, Gabriele had crossed the threshold into Japan with a mix of excitement and determination, ready to embark on a new adventure that would mark important chapter in his career and life. Despite culinary concerns, he was determined to do his best and enjoy this unique experience.

Automitalia's Japanese headquarters occupied an entire three-story building located in Oimachi, residential neighborhood southwest of Tokyo, just off the Yamanote ring. Gabriele's company carried out the production of the components exclusively in Italy, but the building in Oimachi also served as a warehouse for spare parts or for some prototypes waiting to be delivered to customers; therefore, they needed space and could not move to one of the commercial skyscrapers in downtown Tokyo where many of their Asian and American competitors were based. As a result, the office was not a great one: near a train crossing whose signal sounded every five minutes, in a windowless open space, not very comfortable to reach by public transportation.

In contrast to the office, Gabriele had found accommodation in downtown Tokyo that exceeded all his expectations. He had gone perhaps even beyond his planned budget, but the financial sacrifice was, from his point of view, definitely justified. After two weeks of searching, he had found an apartment located on the sixteenth floor of a skyscraper in the Hiroo district, one of the most prestigious and desirable because of its strategic location, close to embassies and within walking distance of Roppongi.

Hiroo was known to be an exclusive residential area in Tokyo, prized especially for its quiet atmosphere and safe environment. The streets were well-maintained and lined with trees, offering a sense of peace and tranquility rare for a large city, even for Tokyo. In addition to Western embassies and supermarkets, the district was home to trendy cafes, fashion boutiques, and international restaurants, making it a vibrant cultural melting pot that attracted expatriates as well as affluent Japanese.

In the evening, moreover, the apartment offered a spectacular view of the illuminated Tokyo Tower. Although the work was exhausting and seemed, living there made everything more bearable.

In the little free time he had, practically only at weekends, he visited the city and became familiar with geography and transportation. He was hardly the kind of person who went out alone at night to meet people; therefore, his only social relationships up to that point had been with fellow students in the basic level Japanese course he attended on Saturday morning.

There he had met Marco, an Italian boy his age, who, like him, had worked a few years in the Italian office of a company in the automotive world and then moved to Japan, only a couple of months before Gabriele.

Marco had heard about the event organized near Tokyo Station and suggested Gabriele to go.

They were to meet directly at the café chosen for the event, so Gabriele left the office a little early, prepared for the evening, and set out for the nearest station, Ebisu Station.

The Yamanote line is one of the busiest train lines in the world. Although on Friday evenings at 8 o'clock it did not reach the peak of morning traffic (when Gabriele had seen with his own eyes the attendants pushing passengers into the trains to get the doors closed), it was still very crowded. Gabriele had to patiently stand in line and wait his turn before he could board the carriage. Nine stops later, he could get off at Tokyo Station in the Chiyoda district, right in front of the Imperial Palace.

He found Tokyo Station particularly unpleasant. It was a huge concrete and steel structure that, although imposing, came across as a cold, non-organized behemoth. The exterior design seemed to attempt to imitate the large train stations of the West but was out of context and out of tune with the surrounding urban landscape. Once inside, the atmosphere did not improve: the corridors were a haphazard maze of intersecting paths with no apparent logic, making navigation confusing and frustrating for the unaccustomed.

The air was permeated with a mixture of smells from the many food stalls scattered around the station, which sold everything from local dishes to quick snacks. These aromas mingled in an uninviting bouquet that permeated clothing and accompanied the traveler well beyond the station exit. The din of commuters' voices, combined with the constant announcements and beeps of arriving and departing trains, created a constant, absorbing background, contributing to the chaotic atmosphere.

The station had been one of the first to be rebuilt after the destruction of the war and had undergone numerous additions to expand and adapt to the increase in rail traffic. However, these expansions seemed to have been done more with urgency than accurate planning, resulting in a complex of additional structures that seemed almost tacked on to the original building without a unifying criterion.

Unlike more modern and well-organized stations such as Shibuya, Shinagawa, or Shinjuku, which boasted clean interfaces, large spaces, and were integrated with luxurious shopping centers and food courts, Tokyo Station lacked these features. Despite its centrality and historical importance, it did not offer the welcoming or efficient experience that could be found in its more up-to- date contemporaries. This contributed to making it a place Gabriele preferred to avoid unless strictly necessary.

Just outside the gates stood the imperial palace with its immense grounds. Every time he saw it, his commercial spirit could not help but be reminded of what he had been told some time earlier, namely that formally dealing with the emperor's private property and considering the size and value of the land in that area, it represented the largest private immobilized capital in the world. In fact, according to some estimates, at the height of the economic boom of the 1990s, the real estate value of the Chiyoda district alone was higher than that of all of Canada.

A few steps from the station exit began the Marunouchi quarter, an example of elegance and sophistication in the heart of Tokyo, surpassed perhaps only by Ginza.

Marunouchi gave him a sense of grandeur, with its wide tree-lined boulevards and gleaming skyscrapers, along with, however, a strange sense melancholy at the emptiness that came with the moment when government offices and corporate headquarters closed and the lights went out on the high floors of the skyscrapers.

On the ground floor of one of these skyscrapers the event would be held.

He found it easily: in addition to Google Maps directions, walking to where the notes Negramaro's 'Estate' came from helped him. An appropriate song for a late September and a little less stereotypical than the 'Volare' he heard in all Italian restaurants at least once a meal. As soon as he entered, he saw Marco together with Hiah, a Korean girl who was taking Japanese class with them; she had nothing to do with Italy but seemed to be person not to miss social event under any circumstances. Already from their attire one could tell who used to evening outings: Gabriele and Marco, almost as if they had agreed beforehand, sported a casual look composed by shorts, All Star shoes and polo shirts, perfect for a relaxed atmosphere. In sharp contrast, Hiah had opted for a more sophisticated outfit appropriate for the evening: she wore a low-cut skirt and blouse that elegantly her figure, and a pair of heels that added a touch of elegance. This, together with her straight, black hair loose over her shoulders, attracted numerous stares, highlighting her skill in adapting his style to the most glamorous occasions.

Gabriele ordered a spritz. He had not had any since his arrival in Japan and, at an event organized by Italians, hoped not to be disappointed.

He was disappointed.

Instead, he found himself holding a white Spritz that tasted more like Soda than anything else, alcohol content probably similar to that of a non-alcoholic beer. Also not to be underestimated was the fact that, with what he had paid for it, he would almost have had dinner in Italy. On the other hand, he was not disappointed with the wheel of Parmigiano and the sliced meats, on which he rushed, having not yet found stores selling good quality ones.

Food was a dilemma that he had only partially solved. When he dined at home it was not a problem, a plate of pasta with tomato sauce he could cook, but when he was out with other people he was in trouble: many restaurants specialized on one type of product, cooked in many different ways. For example, with colleagues he had happened to have lunch at a restaurant that prepared, in every imaginable (and even some unimaginable) way, only eel. He had figured it out by the time they sat down and it was too late.

He was then bingeing on Parmesan and mortadella when Marco called him, in a reproachful tone.

He went over to Marco, standing next to a group of people whom Hiah, speaking in English, was introducing to him: Marta and Davide, a couple of Italian students; Takeshi, manager in a clothing store in Daikanyama who is passionate about Italian fashion; Luna and Hiro, college students of Italian literature and history.

'Luna'. What a peculiar name for a Japanese girl, and what a sweet face, he thought the night before he fell asleep...

TOKYO, JAPAN

Saturday, September 26, 2015

"How peculiar that guy is", Luna thought back as soon as she woke up. She had met him the night before at that aperitivo she had not particularly wanted to attend but which was an excellent opportunity to use her knowledge of Italian language. Going to Italy was too complicated so she had to take advantage of the opportunities that presented themselves in Tokyo.

Fairly tall even by Western standards, light brown hair, clear eyes (in the artificial light she could not tell whether gray or blue), thin, twenty-nine years old, so five years older than her. Not the stereotype of the Italian in the eyes of the Japanese, for whom the Italian by definition was Girolamo Panzetta, an amusing TV personality who was very famous in Japan, muscular, tanned, talkative, flamboyant.

Gabriele had a normal face, he was shy, reserved, attracted by Parmigiano almost more than by Hiah's cleavage. They had exchanged a few words, and she hoped she had not brushed it off with her Italian; then they had said goodbye at the end of the evening without even exchanging WhatsApp contact. However, the group was small, they would definitely see each other again. Now she had to think about studying: the following Monday she would have her Literature exam on Italian Romanticism. Surely Manzoni would have a high chance of being chosen as a question. She had studied it in depth. She had even done a paper on the essay 'Del Romanzo Storico', poking around the differences between the original text and the posthumously published one. However, having to decide what to study for the umpteenth time, she chose the poem "il 5 Maggio", referring to the day of Napoleone death.

"... Manzoni does not care to describe or judge the Napoleon emperor but to interpret the message of his death, which constitutes..."

She stopped, picked up his cell phone and wrote, "Hi Marta, are

we going out tonight?"
She waited three minutes and the cell phone rang.
"Luna? Did they steal your cell phone? You can't be the one asking me out in exam period..."
"Exaggerated!"
"What about your Literature exam?"
"I'm done now, distracting myself will help." Luna replied.
"Bowling in Shibuya?" Marta asked.
"Shall we do darts instead of last time?"
Marta replied with the thumbs-up emoji.
For five minutes Luna turned her cell phone over in her hands.
"Do you also ask the new friends from last night?" Marta's response, full of smiley faces and little hearts, made her realize that her attempt to turn around had been unsuccessful.
Tokyo does not have a city center. There are several city centers depending on one's purpose. The financial center is Marunouchi, headquarters of large companies and the Tokyo government headquarters are in Shinjuku, foreign embassies and nightlife in Roppongi, and so on. For spending an evening with friends, the center of Tokyo is Shibuya.
Luna lived a ten-minute walk from Mitaka Station, west of Shinjuku. It was the typical area for young people with a little job who wanted to live as close to the city center as possible and fit to live in twenty-five square meters, in her case subdivided as follows: a genkan, i.e., an entrance area in which to remove shoes, with an Ikea cabinet to use as a small storage room; a door on the left that led to the bathroom, with the inevitable bathtub, shower, sink, and toilet; an open space with a bed that doubled as a couch (she had abandoned the tradition of sleeping on the tatami spread on the floor), small table on the floor as a dining table, a kitchenette with a single stove, washer and dryer, and refrigerator. Hanging on the walls: television, the indispensable air conditioner, and all kinds of containers. Her pride, however, was the two-by-three-yards small garden accessed through a large French window; there she grew every kind of vegetable she could and even a lemon seedling.

It was small but everything was there, and anyway, with her job as a library assistant, it was the most she could afford.

From Mitaka she was to take the train to Shinjuku for twenty-one minutes, there change for the Yamanote line, and in seven minutes she would arrive in Shibuya.

Taking the A8 exit, Luna arrived at the small square dedicated to Hachiko, the celebrated dog who for years has waited for his owner at that very spot, a classic meeting place for all the inexperienced people in the area. Having to meet up with people who had recently arrived in the city, it seemed the best place to rendezvous. It seemed, however, that all of Tokyo had the same idea that Saturday night.

She picked up the phone, "Moshi moshi! Marta! Where are you?"

"Luna! I can't hear you! Talk louder!"

"Where are you!" shouted Luna.

"In front of Starbucks! I texted you a minute ago!" She closed the call and saw the message she received. Starbucks was across the street, she just had to cross the most iconic intersection in Japan, and perhaps the world. It was not just an intersection, it was a ballet, in which the masses moved like synchronized gears, without intertwining or colliding. It was perhaps the thousandth time she had passed this intersection but each time she wondered how she could arrive to the other side unharmed, and, as every time, she only needed to walk in a straight line at a steady pace to contribute to the dance and find herself safe and sound on the opposite side of the crossing.

"Come, the others are waiting for us at 225", Marta told her as soon as they met.

Dogenzaka 225 was the building in which to play darts, as well as a ramen restaurant on the ground floor (or rather, the first floor, since there was no definition of ground floor in Japan), a nail care center, a beauty salon, and karaoke. Luna was already foretasting the ramen they would have once they finished playing darts....

The place was a regular pub, with three electronic dartboards hanging on the wall so they could play darts. Waiting for them, sitting at the bar drinking beer, were Davide, Marco, Takeshi, and Gabriele. Hiro and Hiah, however, had not been able to come (what a pity...).

After some pleasantries, Marco and Gabriele explained that they had not played darts for at least a decade. The same phrase everyone says when approaching a ping-pong table, a pool table, or a minigolf course.

"I was surprised by this going out to play darts, in Italy that would be impossible," Gabriele said.

"Positively or negatively surprised?" asked Luna. "Positively! I don't like to go out dancing; so having the darts excuse to have a beer and hang out is a great solution. I just need someone to explain the rules..."

"Here I leave the floor to our champion!"

Takeshi took the floor, "Since I spent a good 2,000 yen to buy myself some darts, I guess the champion in question would be me. Here we play 501 which means you start with 501 points and, with each throw, you deduct the points you get. The first one to get exactly 0 has won."

Gabriele was doubtful. Never did he think that, six months later, he would spend twice as many yen to buy his darts.

Thus began an epic match between Luna, Gabriele, Takeshi, and Marco, while Marta and Davide watched. The darts flew in the air as the tension increased with each shot. Marco seemed dominant at first but Luna would not be intimidated. In the end, however, it was Takeshi who surprised everyone with a perfect throw in the triple 20, securing the victory. His jubilation was accompanied by applause and a hint of envy from the other players. Takeshi had demonstrated his impeccable skill.

Two games and two Takeshi wins later (but with less and less distance), the six friends sat at the ramen counter.

Gabriele had discovered ramen only a couple of days after his landing. Finding himself without food, he had entered the first restaurant he spotted along the way. It looked like noodles in broth with chunks of fatty meat thrown into the bowl. He just made sure he didn't get anything fish-based and began to eat. He would only realize later the pleasure a bowl of hot ramen gave on a winter night, but even that late August day, he was pleasantly surprised by the al dente spicy ramen with a garlicky aftertaste. When they finished their snack, they all walked together toward the station, passing through the not very recommendable, at that late hour, neighborhood of Dogenzaka. Luna slowed her pace a little and found herself walking with Gabriele a few dozen feet behind friends.

"Luna is not a typical Japanese name, is it?" asked Gabriele, addressing her directly perhaps for the first time.

"That's right. My mom lived in Italy for a few years and she was so fascinated by your country that she wanted to give me a name in Italian. It's a bit of a problem when I have to spell it because it sounds like 'Runa', however I also like it very much," she replied, smiling.

"It's actually a beautiful name." Luna blushed at Gabriele's affirmation but it was dark and he did not notice. "And have you ever been to Italy?"

"I have been in Milan for few weeks last spring for research on Manzoni. I'm majoring in literature."

"Did you start studying Italian on the advice of your mother?"

"No. She always spoke well Italy to me but I got hooked on the language by listening to the opera in Italian once on the radio. I didn't understand anything but the language sounded beautiful. Even now I don't understand anything if I listen to opera but it still sounds beautiful."

They both headed for the Yamanote line, but while Gabriele had to take it in one direction to go toward Ebisu, Luna had to take it in the opposite direction. They said their goodbyes without even noticing that their friends were gone.

Thirty-two minutes later, Luna was walking home, thinking back annoyed that they had not exchanged cell phone numbers this time either.

She skirted Hiroba-koen, walked a few hundred meters along Kaze-no-sanpomichi (literally, the wind road) and turned right toward Murasaki Bashi dori. She saw the apartment building where she lived after a few dozen feet and, at that moment, her cell phone vibrated: notification from Facebook, the new friend request she had been waiting for.

GENOA, FRENCH EMPIRE

Monday, November 15, 1802

"They'll be here soon, as early as tomorrow morning they could be here", he told her.

"I can't leave, we may never meet again", she answered him, shaking a wisp of fiery red hair from her face.

"You have to do as we said, they can't get their hands on you..."

"... And on the boat, and on the Elixir. I know, I have to go."

"The boat is fast; in a few months you will be safe. They will know of your arrival; everything will be ready. Write to me a letter as soon as you arrive, to tell me you're all right."

"Yes, in a few months... Goodbye..."

"Goodbye..."

IBARAKI, JAPAN

Tuesday, January 15, 2019

Luna was not on duty on Tuesday. After graduating with a degree in Foreign Literature, her dream was to become a teacher but, in the meantime, she worked as an assistant in the Senzoku-Ike library.

She loved her employment. For her, crossing the threshold of the library meant entering an enchanted world, where time seemed to stand still among the shelves filled with volumes. The smell of books mixed with the faint scent of new paper fascinated her every day, and the silence of the reading room offered her a sense of peace and security. Luna was responsible for the fiction section and often organized author meetings and reading workshops for children, finding great satisfaction in seeing visitors' faces light up as they discovered new authors or received personalized advice. Her ability to connect people with the perfect book was well known, and many came to the library specifically for her expert advice.

The library itself was a historic building, with tall windows that let in natural light, illuminating the elegant woodwork and wooden tables scattered throughout the main hall. Located near the picturesque Senzoku-Ike pond, it offered a lovely view of the serene waters, making a perfect backdrop for reading and study. Right next to the library, Senzoku-Ike pond was a true natural jewel in the heart of Tokyo. Surrounded by a lush park with majestic trees and well-maintained path, the lake attracted visitors seeking quiet and natural beauty. Every morning, if she had enough time, Luna chose to go all the way around the lake before entering the library. She loved to cross the small wooden bridge that stretched harmoniously over the calm waters, watching the ducks swimming undisturbed and the petals of the cherry trees resting delicately on the surface in spring.

It took her almost an hour to get to her workplace, but because she did not keep classic office hours, the trains were never too crowded.

Unable to return to Ibaraki on a workday, she had decided to take advantage of that Tuesday off.

The night before, she had looked up the contact of Kiyoshi, her former professor, on her cell phone and sent him a message asking if she could visit the reserved wing of the museum again the next day. Kiyoshi had responded positively, so, that Tuesday morning, Luna had taken the Chuo Line, got off in Tokyo (she did not like that station, too messy, too many stores, very loud announcements...) and taken the Joban Line to her destination.

Returning that evening, she would take a different route: by Mito Line she would arrive in Omiya, her hometown, where she would have dinner with her mother and sister. Then she would probably also stop for the night, since the Wednesday shift would start at 2 p.m., thus giving her plenty of time to return to her home, get ready for work, and arrive at the library on time.

Her sister's name was Emi. It was not a Western name like hers but, even with her, parents had avoided the classic Japanese name. At least for Emi, it was not complicated to spell it with Japanese characters. Emi, with her passion for engineering, had always fascinated Luna. Ever since they were children, they spent hours building strange machines and inventing new games.

Emi's creativity and ingenuity had added a touch of magic to their childhood.

Although their academic paths were different, Luna and Emi shared an unbreakable bond and a complicity that only sisters can understand. With each homecoming, Luna looked forward to soaking in the cozy familiarity of Omiya and spending precious time with her beloved sister.

Emi was twenty-two years old and would soon become an engineer. Not that in Japan degree course defined career possibilities as in Western nations: a Humanities graduate could very well become an engineer at Toyota, and a Construction Engineering graduate could make a career in finance, much more easily than in Europe. More than the address, it was the name of the university they had attended that made the difference.

Comparing with her Italian friends, she had realized that in Japan it was very difficult to get into the prestigious universities that then gave access to the best jobs and with the greatest career prospects however, once you got in, the course of study was almost just a formality. At job interviews, potential employers would first ask what university they attended and only then, but not always, what the major was. In addition, the bond between university classmates remained close throughout the working career, further facilitating the creation of leadership teams from the same school.

In Italy it was almost the opposite: free entry into the university (except for special cases) and then a battle on every single exam. During the time when they were hanging out with Gabriele, Marco and the other friends, Emi was also sometimes part of the group, but in the late period, and especially after the dramatic spring of 2017, she had drifted away to spend time with her peers.

However, she had also stayed in touch with her Italian friends, and Luna had mentioned to her about the Italian flag of the 1800s and how she used it as an excuse for a chat with Gabriele. That evening she would update her on possible new clues she hoped to find at the museum.

The trip on the Joban Line to Ibaraki took more than two hours. She had found a window seat and, leaning his head against the glass, watched the landscape transform. Luna's train ride from Tokyo to Ibaraki offered a fascinating glimpse of the urban and rural Japanese landscape. In the first fifteen minutes, the train snaked through the beating heart of Tokyo, where luxurious apartment buildings stood proud under the sky, with the Tokyo Skytree dominating the skyline, majestic and imposing. The morning light reflected off the glass surfaces of the buildings, creating plays of light that danced rapidly out the windows of the moving train.

As the vehicle left the city center, the landscape began

to transform. Luxurious buildings were giving way to more modest structures, with more popular, close-knit apartment buildings. Although the design of the buildings became less sophisticated, one thing remained the same: the orderliness and cleanliness of the streets and neighborhoods. Luna noted how, despite the relatively less affluence of the inhabitants of these areas, there was no sign of neglect or decadence in the common areas.

Foreigners visiting Tokyo were surprised by the cleanliness of the parks, the punctuality of the trains, the kindness of the people, but Luna was convinced that it was the suburbs where one could appreciate the true spirit of the Japanese citizen, when they took care of the common areas without being constrained there by their work or the desire to appear in front of others, doing it because they knew that this was right and therefore this is how it should be done, just out of self-respect.

Continuing the journey, the train slowly passed the dense urbanization, giving way to vast open spaces. Bright green rice fields stretched to the horizon, interspersed with small farms and cherry trees, which exploded into a triumph of pink color in spring. Small villages dotted the landscape, with traditional Japanese houses and meticulously tended gardens. The contrast between the hectic activity of the metropolis and the serenity of the Japanese countryside was striking and fascinating, offering Luna a moment of reflection and admiration for the diversity and beauty of the scenery that flowed before her eyes as she approached her destination.

When the landscape gave way to the actual countryside, she squinted her eyes and fell asleep.

TOKYO, JAPAN

Thursday, November 12, 2015

In the contract to expatriate to Japan, Gabriele had obtained several benefits, ironically through the person who least desired his presence in Japan.

Before Gabriele's arrival, Automitalia's Japanese branch was run exclusively by local staff, including the general manager, Watanabe-san. The latter maintained an almost dictatorial control over the office, seeing himself as an absolute ruler of all Automitalia's operations in Japan. The idea of welcoming an envoy from headquarters was a source of irritation to him, perceiving the new figure almost as an emissary sent to oversee its activities.

Consequently, unable to openly voice his opposition, Watanabe adopted a subtly obstructive tactic. When asked from Italy for an estimate of the cost of relocating the new employee, he deliberately listed every possible expense, inflating the costs to stratospheric levels in the hope of discouraging the central office from embarking on this course of action.

However, Watanabe had not foreseen that the officials he was in contact with lacked autonomous decision-making power and merely uncritically included all the figures he provided in the expatriation budget. In this way, the measures he had thought might be a deterrent turned, without his knowledge, into a series of additional benefits for Gabriele.

To his delight, Gabriele then found himself budgeted at the highest possible level: apartment in downtown Tokyo, company car reimbursement, two fully paid returns to Italy each year, cable TV, in-room laundry service and, a particularly welcome benefit, Japanese lesson once a week.

As with all Thursday mornings, the teacher would go directly to the office for a two-hour course during working hours (thanks again, Watanabe san).

Japanese writing consists of three main si- stems of characters:

katakana, hiragana, and kanji. Katakana and hiragana both consist of forty-six characters that represent the same syllables but differ in their graphic forms.

Katakana is characterized by angular lines and a simple graphic structure, making it ideal for transcribing foreign words, names of non-Japanese origin, onomatopoeic sounds, and technical or scientific terms. This system has a sharper, geometric appearance, imparting a feeling of clarity and precision.

Hiragana, on the other hand, is known for its curvilinear forms and is mainly used for writing native Japanese words and grammatical elements such as verb desinences and particles. This writing system offers a visually softer and more fluent appearance than katakana, making it easy to read texts entirely in Japanese.

First, Gabriele had memorized the katakana characters, which was essential when one wanted to order in restaurants since all foreign dishes were written on menus using this system.

Then he had switched to hiragana, with which he could begin to write a few words.

That Thursday morning, he would begin with the teacher to tackle the dreaded kanji.

The teacher began by explaining that kanji had a rich and complex history. Originally derived from Chinese characters, they were introduced to Japan around the fifth century CE. During the following centuries, the kanji writing system had been independently adapted and expanded, with new kanji created to represent Japanese concepts and words. This development had led to the peculiar situation in which kanji could be read as in the Chinese original but also as the Japanese word they represented.

For example, the kanji 山, meaning "mountain," can be read as "san" in the pronunciation of Chinese origin or as "yama" in the native Japanese reading. The choice of reading depends on the context: when the kanji is used as a stand-alone noun, it reads "yama", while when it is part of a mountain name, it reads "san" (e.g., Fujisan, Mount Fuji). After realizing this subtlety,

Gabriele began to avoid Japanese restaurants called Fuji-yama, a term that sounds terribly incorrect to Japanese ears.

Over the centuries, the kanji system had been standardized, with a set of about 2,000 basic characters, known as Joyo Kanji, that were commonly used in modern writing. Currently, there were about 2,100 kanji in the Joyo Kanji list, which were considered fundamental to the understanding and writing of the modern Japanese language. Anway, there were thousands of other kanji not included in this list, which were used in more specialized or less common contexts.

In Japanese schools, kanji were taught gradually, with students beginning to learn them in elementary and middle school. The learning of the kanji was a fundamental part of Japanese education and required years of practice and constant study. Students usually learned to read and write kanji throughout their schooling, focusing on an increasing number of characters according to their level of schooling.

Learning kanji was a challenge for Japanese and foreign students, requiring time, dedication and constant practice. However, once students had acquired a solid foundation of kanji, they could benefit greatly from their ability to understand and communicate in Japanese in a more sophisticated and accurate way.

They then began with the basic words: 'person,' 人, which represented a stylized person. It then switched to 'big,' 大, which represented a person with outstretched arms, thus indicating the concept of big.

More complex kanji could be composed of radicals, that is primitive kanji that depicted basic concepts necessary to arrive at the more complex meaning.

For example, the teacher explained to him, the radical of 'water' was 氵; this radical could be found in so many words having to do with the concept of 'water,' for example 'pond' 池 or 'sea' 海. Other examples, which led to the story of ancient Japan, could be: 'home' 家 which was formed by the radicals 宀 'roof' and 豕 'pig' thus indicating that, in the past, it was considered home to be the place where a pig stay under the roof; or 'forest' 森 which was formed by the repetition three times of the radical of 'tree' 木: so many 'trees' equals 'forest'.

Gabriele was fascinated by these explanations: he was sure that he would never be able to memorize more than about fifty kanji but the logic with which they were constructed fascinated him, like the rebuses he used to solve in the evening on the Puzzle Week he received every week from Italy.

The two hours ended as always too soon. He made an appointment for the following week and returned to his desk.

PAVIA, HOLY ROMAN EMPIRE

Friday, March 27, 1789

In the quiet academic scene of Pavia, a man of rare intelligence and profound erudition had been established for years. The Professor, as his colleagues and students respectfully called him, was a respected and well-known figure within academic circles. Dressed in understated elegance, his manner was composed and reserved, but behind those dark, searching eyes was a mind fertile with thoughts and ideas. He was a middle-aged man with lightly backcombed dark hair and a face furrowed with wrinkles that told stories of past experiences.

The Professor was a constant presence in the corridors of the University, where his lectures fascinated and inspired the most promising students. His erudition knew no bounds, and his contribution to scientific knowledge was known throughout the kingdom, including the palace of the emperor, who knew him directly.

A convinced bachelor, the Professor occasionally indulged in the luxury of attending soirees of the local nobility, where the conversation was as rich in insights as the delicious courses served at the table. He was a keen observer and a brilliant speaker, able to juggle the various social circles with ease.

Although his name was on everyone's lips, the Professor maintained a certain aura of mystery, as if there was always something more to be discovered beneath the surface of his apparent normality. Yet behind that mask of secrecy was a man of extraordinary talent and deep humanity, ready to leave an indelible mark on the history of science and knowledge.

That evening, the Professor had a social outing planned. As the sun set on the horizon, tinging the sky with shades of orange and pink, he carefully prepared himself, wearing his best suit and expertly adjusting the knot of his tie. It was not often that the Professor left the rigor of his study to immerse himself in the lively theatrical atmosphere of Pavia, but that evening he felt the uncontrollable desire to be carried away by the magic of the show.

The theater was a sumptuous white stone building, with its majestic columns and gilded decorations shining in candlelight. The doors opened to welcome audiences eager to escape from the daily monotony and immerse themselves in the enchanted stories that would to life on the stage.

Inside, the atmosphere was electric, with voices mingling with the rustling of clothes and the clinking of silver cutlery. The Professor was immersed in this vortex of conflicting emotions as he searched his eyes his place among the crowd eager to watch the performance of 'The Barber of Seville, or the Useless Precaution,' a comic opera composed some fifteen years earlier by Pierre-Augustin de Beaumarchais that told how the cunning barber Figaro helped Count Almaviva win the love of the young Rosina, despite Bartolo's vain efforts to protect her.

Sitting in his chair, the Professor let the excitement of the show envelop him completely: the lights were dimming and the curtain was slowly rising on the stage.

As the play came to life on the stage, the Professor was carried away by the enchanted atmosphere of the theater. His eyes rested on the actors dancing and acted with grace and talent, but it was one particular figure on stage that caught his attention.

It was she, Rosina, the actress who played the role of the youthful and vivacious heroine of 'The Barber of Seville.' The Professor was enchanted by her stage presence and her ability to bring the character to life with such naturalness and grace.

Among the comedy scenes and love entanglements, the Professor recognized some of the most famous lines in the work. When Rosina performed the famous aria 'Una voce poco fa', the Professor was enraptured by the beauty and expressiveness of her voice, which filled the theater with emotion and pathos. It was not only her prowess as an actress that captivated the Professor. It was something more, intensity in her gaze, a passion in her handling of words and emotions, that struck him deeply. In that moment, the Professor felt that there was something special about that woman, something that went beyond mere theatrical acting, and his curiosity was captured by his magnetic presence on stage.

After the performance, as the Professor stood in the foyer of the theater, an elegant figure approached him with decisive passion. It was she, the actress who had played Rosina so masterfully.

"That was an extraordinary performance," said the Professor with a polite smile, trying to hide his surprise at seeing the actress so close to him. "What is your name?"

"You may call me Rosina," smiled the actress. "Thank you for the compliment, Professor," she added with a slight bow, giving away that she recognized him; her gaze scanned the Professor's face with an intensity that did not escape his keen eye. As she moved, a cascade of fire-red hair shone in the light of the foyer, drawing the gaze of anyone nearby. This detail surprised the Professor who did not expect the Rosina of the stage to have such vibrant and distinctive hair.

The Professor felt intrigued by her presence and lively intelligence. In that brief meeting, he felt a subtle bond uniting them, an understanding that went beyond words and fueled mutual curiosity.

As the days passed, the bond between the Professor and Rosina deepened more and more. Every time they met, they found new topics of conversation ranging from science to literature, from politics to art. The Professor began to consider Rosina not only a brilliant actress, but also a fellow traveler in his search for truth and knowledge. At the same time, Rosina felt more and more attracted to the Professor's curious spirit and kindness, finding in him a valuable ally in his desire to explore new horizons.

Over time, their relationship grew into something deeper and more meaningful. Every day, Rosina felt more and more connected to the Professor, longing to spend more time with him and to share every aspect of his life.

So it was that, one day, Rosina made a decision that would change the course of her life. She determined to stay in Pavia, leaving the theater company to continue the love and scientific re- lection with the Professor. It was not an easy choice but she knew it was the right one for her.

As the days passed, as their love affair deepened, the Professor and Rosina also began to explore new territories, those of science and knowledge. Through long and passionate conversations, they exchanged ideas, theories and plans, fueling their curiosity desire to discover the wonders of the world around them. So it was that the Professor and Rosina found themselves in his study, surrounded by books and scientific instruments. It was time to kick off their scientific adventure, to put their brilliant minds to the test and explore new horizons together.

With patience and determination, the Professor guided Rosina through the meanders of physics and mathematics, explaining complex concepts to her with simplicity and clarity. Rosina, for her part, eagerly grasped every new idea, displaying a keen mind and an extraordinary ability to learn.

Together, they engaged in experiments and observations, testing their theories and seeking answers to the deepest questions of the universe. There was no limit to their thirst for knowledge, and every day was a new adventure, an opportunity to discover something unexpected and wonderful.

And so, as the Professor and Rosina went deeper and deeper into the world of science, their relationship was transformed into something even deeper and more meaningful. In addition to the love that united them, there was now also an intellectual connection that bound them together, a bond made up of curiosity, discovery, and a passion for knowledge.

IBARAKI, JAPAN

Tuesday, January 15, 2019

Luna got off at Mito station. From there, the Prefectural Museum of History could be reached in about forty minutes on foot. It was noon, she had an appointment with Kiyoshi at 2 p.m., so she had plenty of time to have lunch and take a walk.

She would have liked to eat by ocean but would have wasted too much time. Fortunately, right next to the station was Senba Lake.

The previous week had passed very quickly by the lake and she had promised herself that she would visit it at the next opportunity; now she made herself a further promise: she would have to return at the end of March, during the hanami period. Indeed, on the north side of the lake flowed a stream called Sakura-kawa, 'river of cherry trees'. The stream was only three or four yards wide and completely lined with cherry trees that stretched out their branches toward the waterway, reaching up to touch each other. They would have created a unique spectacle at the time of blossoming. She could not help but cast her mind back April 2017, to that walk with Gabriele in Roppongi.

After a few hundred meters she crossed the Sakura-kawa on a small pedestrian bridge and arrived at Senba park, where she sat at a picnic table. The lake reminded her a lot of the one in Senzoku-Ike, next to the library where she works. Here, too, the stillness of the body of water was accompanied by bare cherry trees waiting to show their full splendor after a few weeks, swan-shaped boats sailing quietly through the park, employees of local businesses eating their lunch outside enjoying the cool sunny day.

She took out of the bag the tonkatsu sandwich, breaded and fried pork meat, that she had bought at the station and enjoyed her lunch while waiting for her appointment.

At 2 p.m. sharp, she stood at the entrance to the museum, immersed in a vast park that amplified its solemnity. The building had a singular structure, composed of three main bodies with radically different architectural styles that seemed to narrate different eras.

The first building was imposing and austere: squared off, with gray bricks and equipped with only a couple of small windows that made it resemble a medium-sized fortress, almost symbolizing strength and stability.

The second, on other hand, was a completely different structure: it was built of wood, spread over two floors, with large windows and porches that made it resemble a 19th century European colonial house. Its lines were soft and cozy, in sharp contrast to the severity of the former.

The third building, toward which he headed, was an example of classical Japanese architecture, probably dating from the late Edo period. With its elegant, curved roof and finely crafted wooden structures, it represented an era of refined aesthetics and culture.

At the entrance she found Kiyoshi waiting for her. "Hello Kiyoshi-san! Thank you for allowing me to return so soon!"

"Hello Luna-chan! Of course, you are always welcome! Also, I was intrigued by your message. What is it that you found so interesting?"

"Come let me show you, you won't believe it!"

"I'm sorry but I just can't right now, I'm busy for at least an hour. Come by when you finish telling me about it."

"Certainly! Can I take pictures?"

Kiyoshi looked at her with a puzzled look. "The room you want to visit contains documents from the 18th and 19th centuries that are not particularly secret... Go ahead and take pictures but remember to mention the museum in case of publication." He smiled. "Anyway, you have made me even more curious, see you later."

"Certainly!" replied Luna.

She entered the building and found herself in the main room of the part of the museum devoted to the Edo period, when the Toku- gawa clan ruled that area and virtually all of present-day

Japan.

An exhibition devoted to the development of reverberatory furnaces in Japan was being held at that time.

She crossed the hall, took a staircase to the basement, and found himself in a hallway with several doors. She knew which one she had to open. She entered and, with excitement, picked up the folder she had looked at the previous week.

The room was rather dark and gloomy, about three by four meters, with metal shelves along the entire length except for a small table with a chair and a lamp, since the light from the only bulb in the room was very dim and, in any case, covered by the shelves. It was clear that was used for storage of not too valuable materials. Who knows if indeed the drape he had seen had ended up there by mistake and actually belonged to a much more recent era.

The piece of cloth was there, she could make no mistake, it was an Italian flag. The green was darker than what she had in mind, it was perhaps more of an emerald green. The white was yellowed and the red was pink, normal to have faded a bit after more than two centuries. But the certainty that it was an Italian flag also came from the lettering that could be discerned. There were three lines in the center white band. On the first line was the word 'Lombardia.' In fact, no, the word was 'Lombarda', without the 'i'. Below was another text, which was difficult to read. Perhaps the sentence on the second line ended with '...turi' and the third with '...alio'.

On the back, again the Italian flag, obviously in reversed colors: red on the left, white in the middle and green on the right. No writing printed on the fabric but, looking closely, there was a glimpse of something added by hand. 'Paris'. Paris? Luna just couldn't put that information together: Italian flag, Lombardy, Paris. She took pictures of the front and back and sent them to Gabriele, adding, "Kiyoshi-san told me I can take pictures but I can't publish them. Don't send them to anyone!!!"

Then she took the note that was in the same envelope as the flag. The text said what she had already told Gabriele: 'filed in the fourth year of Bunka's reign,' as well other notes that he had not felt urgent to communicate to Gabriele, for example, that the object had been found at the home of Shoya (the village chief) in Choshi, small village in the far southeast of Japan, about three hours by train from where he was, and that the object was described as blue, white, and pink. The blue could easily have been mistaken for emerald green. Or was it really blue and was that a French flag? Luna was certain it was Italian: the color was definitely green and the word 'Lombarda' confirmed it. Of course, that wording 'Paris,' however, could have raised some doubts. Then she remembered that Italy had only united around 1860. Could there have been an Italian flag before that date?

She also sent Gabriele the photo of the note, adding the translation of the text: 'Bunka kunen yon-nen kakusu sareta' means 'filed in the fourth year...' Luna paused. She looked at the note again: the text was faded, the characters written were in the handwriting of two hundred years earlier, and it seemed to have been quickly drafted, lacking some hiragana necessary for correct grammar (the sentence should have been 'Bunka no kunen ni yon-nen ni kakusu sareta') however, the general meaning was understandable. However, she could not be one hundred percent sure of the meaning of the text; in fact, she realized that there might be a different interpretation. Finding herself in a museum she had assumed that 'Kakusu' was used with the meaning of 'to file' but, lacking the hiragana necessary for an unambiguous interpretation, it could also have the meaning of 'to hide.' So the phrase could have meant 'Hidden in the fourth year of Bunka's reign' which then could easily have continued with 'from Choshi's Shoya.' So the Shoya of Choshi could have hidden that flag. Hidden from whom? The Shoya was the head of the village, so he could only have been afraid of some higher authority (someone close to the Satake clan that ruled that area at that time), who then found the item, filed it away, and it happened to be 200 years later in a folder of documents about collections and tributes in a small room of a suburban museum.

It was a fascinating hypothesis!

She wrote everything to Gabriele but could not expect a reply soon. He would have been in the office at that time, likely to reply to her in the Japanese evening, during the Italian lunch break.

She rushed out and looked for Kiyoshi to ask him for advice as well. She tried to call him on his cell phone but, after six rings, she ended the call. She could have asked the concierge where to look for him but realized she did not have too much time since she had to go to her sister Emi's. In fact, no, she could not go. She was too curious. She had to run to the village of Choshi to see the place where the flag had been found.

She planned in her mind and executed quickly.

First, a message for Kiyoshi. "Kiyoshi-san! It's more interesting than I thought: I found an early 19th century Italian flag that a Shoya had probably tried to hide from the Satake clan! I'm going to Choshi (the Shoya's town) tonight, I'll come back this way as soon as I can, and if you have time, I'll tell you all about it!"

Second: "Moshi moshi Emi-chan!"

"Hello Luna-chan, are you coming?"

"No, look, happened..." She told her what she was doing, that she had heard from Gabriele, that she was planning to spend the night in Choshi and would come by the next day.

"I'll just pop in quickly, just to say hello to you and Mom, who I have to be at work at 4 o'clock."

"Fine, I'll eat all Oyaku-Don that Mom made!"

Third, booking a hotel in Choshi.

Fourth: "Moshi moshi buchō-san."

"Moshi moshi Luna-san, are you okay?"

"Yes, boss, everything is fine. Can I ask you a favor?" asked Luna to her supervisor at the Senzoku-Ike Library.

"Try..."

"Tomorrow morning I would like to visit the library in Choshi. I saw on their website that they also have a section devoted to historical documents but you can only enter with permission. Wouldn't you have any contacts that would allow me to take a look?"

"Is it for research on the Satake clan?"

"That's right, I may have found something very interesting!"

"So, listen," replied his manager. "The research is important for the library; we want to make a good impression. Don't come tomorrow, devote proper time to this work. I'll try to call Choshi's library manager now and let you know."

"Thank you very much buchō-san!"

Luna arrived in Choshi at 7 p.m. and first headed to the Choshi Plaza Hotel, a business hotel near the station, the most convenient he had found. The room, like all hotels in Japan, and particularly business hotels, was small and spartan, but Luna had a pleasant surprise. The room offered a wonderful view of the Choshi Bashi, the suspension bridge that connected the mainland to the long, thin island of Kamisu. It would have been a wonderful tourist area had it not been for the Japanese's lack of interest in beaches and the fact that it overlooked not a calm inland sea but the frigid and dangerous Pacific Ocean. She got lost for a few minutes admiring the colorful lights of the Choshi Bashi, then decided to go out for dinner.

She was happy to dine in the Chiba region, where the typical food was one of her favorite dishes, Somen Nagashi, a variety of noodles with very thin noodles. It was a cold dish, not the best for a mid-January evening, but she had never tried this dish in her home place and she had to.

She then headed to a restaurant specializing in that cuisine.

She sat at the counter, in front of a bamboo rod on which flowed noodles for patrons to pick up with chopsticks. They were then dipped into the available sauces and brought to their mouths. Damn Gabriele: because of him, she no longer enjoyed them as much as she used to. She remembered when she had been with him at a restaurant in Somen Nagashi in Tokyo and he had expressed his doubts about the hygiene of that kind of service. She had never paid attention to it before but, now, seeing other people put chopsticks in their mouths and then in the water that brought her noodles, it made her uncomfortable.

She received a message on her cell phone. Maybe it was Gabriele who answered her message, but it was her boss confirming her free access to any room in the Choshi Library the next day as early as the first morning. "Well done, boss," she thought, "and damn Gabriele."

BERGAMO, ITALY

Tuesday, January 15, 2019

Gabriele saw the message during working hours, but that was a complicated day.

On that Tuesday, the meetings overlapped as if he could divide himself into several self-sufficient entities. He had no problems handling significant workloads and responsibilities but attending multiple meetings at the same time was not physically possible for him.

At work, the situations that gave him the most anxiety were those in which he had to overlap commitments, and that day it had already happened to him twice to mute a call with one client to talk on his cell phone with another, having to pay attention to both.

Since he had returned to Italy, he had a more operative role and in more markets than his responsibilities in Japan. It was called 'horizontal growth'.

This growth, however, had brought him into territory in which he was not comfortable as he was more in contact with situations that could not be controlled, for example, quality or non-availability of parts for customers, situations for which he was responsible but which he could not directly manage...

Gabriele liked to calculate costs and prices, plan and long-term activities, analyze specifications, and discuss with clients the best ways to achieve common goals. Then these crazy variables would come along and everything would blow up.

During days like those, as soon as he had a free moment he would get away, he would think that in the evening he would fix all the bugs in his video game, he would publish it, he would become rich and could have stopped working in the office. That thought for a moment filled his brain with endorphins, just enough so that he could return to focus on work problems with less tension, so much so that he had a very solid alternative plan to survive!

Once the emergencies were over (unresolved, of course, only postponed to the next day) and after finally being able to do the work he had not been able to complete during the day because of the constant emergencies, he had a habit of staying a final ten minutes in the office to relax, a necessity similar to that of divers slowly rising to the surface.

Arriving home late, he was almost about to forget Luna's message but, after dinner, he looked carefully at what he had only given a quick glance at during the day.

Yes, that was an Italian flag and it said 'Lombarda'.

It took him only a little while to verify what it was: he opened the Wikipedia page about the Italian flag and there it was, an exact copy of the image he had received from Luna. The text on the flag in Wikipedia allowed him to read correctly the faded lettering present on the flag of Ibaraki: 'Legione Lombarda, Cacciatori a Cavallo'.

It was thus the flag of the 'Legione Lombarda', a military unit of the Army of Italy formed by Napoleon Bonaparte during the Italian campaign in 1796.

Until the last decade of the 18th century, Northern Italy was a patchwork of states and territories under the control of various European powers. The region consisted mainly of the Kingdom of Sardinia, the Duchy of Milan, the Republic of Venice, the Duchy of Modena, the Duchy of Parma and Piacenza, and the Grand Duchy of Tuscany, in addition to territories under the direct influence of the Austro-Hungarian Empire. This political fragmentation made the region a target for the French revolutionary powers, who sought to export the principles of the Revolution.

In 1792, revolutionary France declared war on Austria, beginning a series of conflicts that would disaggregate Europe. The situation in Italy remained relatively stable until 1796, when the young general Napoleon Bonaparte was appointed commander of the Army of Italy. Napoleon's Italian campaign marked the beginning of a series rapid and decisive French victories.

In 1796, Napoleon Bonaparte launched his campaign against the Austro-Hungarian forces and their allies in northern Italy. His brilliant and daring strategy enabled him to achieve consecutive victories, rapidly changing the course of the war. One of the first significant battles was the Battle of Montenotte, where Napoleon defeated the Piedmontese forces. This success paved the way for further victories against the Austro-Hungarians.

Subsequent victories, such as the Battle of Lodi, on May 10, 1796, saw Napoleon bend the Austrian army, allowing it to enter Milan. The Battle of Arcole, fought Nov. 15-17, 1796, was another key victory for Napoleon, which consolidated French control over the region. French forces continued to win decisive victories, culminating in the Battle of Rivoli in Jan. 1797, which secured French dominance over much of northern Italy.

During these campaigns, many cities and territories changed hands, moving from Austro-Hungarian to French control. The proclamation of the Cisalpine Republic in 1797 marked a significant turning point. The Cisalpine Republic, encompassing much of northern Italy, became a satellite state of France, with Napoleon exercising a considerable influence on its politics and governance. On October 17, 1797, the signing of the Treaty of Campoformio between France and Austria officially sanctioned territorial changes, recognizing French sovereignty over many regions in northern Italy. The treaty dismantled the Venetian Republic, ceding its territories to Austria in exchange for the recognition of French conquests in Lombardy and the Cisalpine Republic. The leading rulers of the time included Victor Amadeus III of Savoy, king of Sardinia, and Francis II of Asburg-Lorraine, emperor of the Holy Roman Empire. In France, Napoleon Bonaparte was beginning to emerge as a dominant figure, destined to profoundly influence the course of European history.

Therefore, the Ibaraki flag could not be dated before 1796 and, between that date and 1807, this flag had arrived in Japan. It continued to seem impossible.

The flag came from northwestern Italy; if it had indeed arrived in Japan in the early 19th century, it could only have arrived there by ship from Liguria.

He looked at the second photo sent by Luna: the back of the flag and the words 'Paris'. The flag was indeed that of a military unit of the French army, so there had to be a connection to France. He looked closer at the picture and noticed marks to the left of the word 'Paris'. might have been another word but he could not read what it might say.

He downloaded the photo to his pc and loaded it into an image-processing program. He selected the 'Remove Background' option and, going patiently to select the areas to keep and those to remove, he had confirmation that there were other letters before the word 'Paris,' however, absolutely illegible.

In his role at work, he also occasionally did communications and marketing, so he had much more efficient image processing software than the free program he had at home.

He sent the image to his office email: he would try again the next day.

KAMAKURA, JAPAN

Sunday, March 13, 2016

For the first Sunday of clear weather, the group decided to take a trip to Kamakura. Gabriele had never been there and was curious to visit a city so small but so important to Japan's history.

In the 12th century, Kamakura, a coastal town in the Kanto region, southwest of present-day Tokyo, arose as the political and spiritual center of Japan. Dominated by majestic mountains and washed by the ocean, this town soon became the centerpiece of the powerful Minamoto shogunate. The first shogun, Minamoto no Yoritomo, established his government here, turning Kamakura into a crossroads of culture, politics and the arts, essentially the capital of ancient Japan.

As time passed, Kamakura became the stage for political intrigue and clashes among the various samurai factions. Zen temples and Shinto shrines flourished, coexisting with samurai dwellings and bustling markets.

One of Kamakura's most famous temples was Tokeiji Temple, famous for its historical role as a refuge for women fleeing abusive or unsatisfactory marriages and seeking divorce. Founded in 1285 by Kakusan-ni, widow of the regent Hōjō Tokimune, the temple was a Buddhist convent of the Rinzai school of Zen Buddhism.

Women seeking divorce could repair to the Tokeiji and, after a three-year stay, had the legal right to obtain a divorce from their husbands, without the need for their consent. This unique right gave the temple a significant role in protecting women's rights at a time when divorce was extremely difficult for the female gender to obtain.

With the end of the 12th century, the town fell into disrepair due to internal strife and was abandoned, resurrecting only in the modern era as a tourist attraction, thanks to its temples, gardens but also (and that was the main purpose of the group's trip that day) as an area for surfing enthusiasts, thanks to its wide beach overlooking the ocean.

Gabriele was not very comfortable: he had no problem with sea sports, having even had good placings at the junior national sailing championships in the past (the cup for second place in the 2006 Olbia regattas was displayed prominently on the nightstand in his Hiroo apartment), but surfing was something else. It seemed to require a musculature and balance that he felt he did not possess. Then was the topic of 'bathing in the ocean in winter' but Luna had convinced him by explaining that, in addition to boards, they would rent suits. It had sounded like a good solution to him but, now that the time was approaching, he had lost all confidence.

So, the schedule was decided: departure at dawn, morning surfing, afternoon visiting temples, and return to Tokyo for dinner.

Gabriele, Luna, Davide, Marta, and Hiro had met in Shinagawa. They would find the rest of the group (Marco, Hiah and Takeshi) directly in Kamakura.

The eight friends met at a Chokokro chain establishment in a small shopping center across the street from the beach. The chain was not really called Chokokro but St. Marc. Café however, their brioche pastries were so good (basically, brioche dough rolled around a whole chocolate bar) that their name (indeed, Chokokro) had, for the small group of friends, identified the chain.

From the venue they could see a cloudy sky from which a shy late winter sun was trying to break through, and beyond the wide sandy beach, a sea rough but not too much, ideal for first surfing trials.

After breakfast, they set out for the hut where they had reserved their equipment. Before them were three pairs of boys, probably also at their very first experiences. Evidently that was a good day to start trying, and this reassured Gabriele.

Of their group, the only expert turned out to be Takeshi, who evidently played other sports besides darts. It then fell to him to translate the manager's explanations. The translation frustrated

Gabriele in exactly the same way that the translations of his colleagues during business meetings were frustrating: three minutes of speech in Japanese were translated with few words. It turned out, therefore, that the only explanation needed to be able to surf, after a lengthy explanation, was, "Lie down on the board, paddle out to sea, stand up on the board when the wave comes."

The next two hours were among the most strenuous of his life. It was not that he was totally out of practice, but that continuous rowing lying on his belly required muscles that he simply did not have. For the first hour and a half, he could not even stand up for a few seconds, then the situation changed: without understanding what was going on, he found himself upright on the board and began to float on the back of the wave. Those few seconds seemed like minutes to him, the fatigue vanished in the face of that moment of pure gratification.

When the two hours were over, they returned to shore. He did not even make it to the store. On the shoreline he slumped on the sand, supine, the board beside him, breathless, eyes closed, cold sun on his skin, smile on his lips.

A few seconds later, he felt a shadow on his face, as if a cloud had covered the sun. He opened his eyes and saw Luna's face a few inches from his own. What beautiful eyes she had. At that moment he realized what made his eyes so special compared to typical Japanese eyes: those small creases below the lower lash line that gave her gaze an almost smiling look.

"You did great! Did you have a good time?"

"Very much, but what a struggle! I saw that you were comfortable instead!"

"For me it was already the second time, the next time will be much better for you too."

At lunch they went to a shirasu-don restaurant, a new experience for Gabriele.

With a certain curiosity, he approached the plate of rice delicately laid under a blanket of shining white fish. The shirasu looked like little gems of the sea. With a light touch of his chopsticks, he savored the first bite, experiencing a combination of delicate sea flavors and the simplicity and sweetness of rice.

After lunch, just to completely run out of energy for the day, they decided to take a walk to the Great Buddha.

The Great Buddha of Kamakura, known locally as 'Kamakura Daibutsu,' was one of Japan's most significant and impressive icons. This historical monument represented one of the largest bronze Buddha statues in the country and was a tangible testimony to Japan's rich history and deep spirituality. The statue of the Great Buddha stood imposingly inside the Kotokuin Temple, located near Kamakura Station. Made of gilded bronze, the seated Buddha measured over thirteen meters in height and weighed about ninethy-three tons. Its imposing presence dominated the surrounding landscape, emanating a feeling of calm and majesty.

The statue represented Amida Buddha, the Buddhist deity associated with compassion and universal salvation. The Buddha was depicted seated in a meditative posture, with his hands placed on his knees and his eyes half-closed in an expression of inner peace. The intricate details of his serene expression and draped robes testified to the craftsmanship of the master sculptors who had created that marvel.

As they walked in the direction of the Buddha, Hiro told his Italian friends the story of the statue.

"The Great Buddha of Kamakura has a rich and fascinating history dating back to the 13th century. It was commissioned in 1252 by Shogun Hojo Tokiyori, one of the most powerful rulers of the time, with the aim of promoting the spread of Buddhism in medieval Japan. The original statue was housed inside a large wooden temple but was destroyed by an earthquake in the 15th century. Since then, the Buddha has withstood numerous natural disasters and catastrophes, becoming a symbol of resilience and spirituality for the Japanese people."

Hiro continued.

"One of the most striking features of the Great Buddha of Kamakura is its inner bell, which is said to have the power to bring good luck to those who ring it. Visitors can access the inside of the statue through a narrow spiral staircase and give the bell a gentle tapping, hoping to attract good luck and prosperity into their lives."

Having all attention of his friends, he continued, "Another fascinating anecdote concerns the Buddha's nose, which is said to have been rebuilt several times over the centuries. Se- cording to legend, the statue once had a more pronounced nose, but it was damaged by an earthquake and was never again fully restored. Today, the nose of the Great Buddha is slightly flat, giving it an air of mystery and charm."

They arrived at the temple and the statue appeared in all its majesty.

First, they queued up for a greeting to the temple's patron gods with the procedure that everyone was now familiar with: washing hands with a small wooden ladle, tossing a coin, two hand claps, and a slight bow.

Finally, they climbed the stairs inside the giant statue. Gabriele gave the bell a little tug as, out of the corner of his eye, he looked at Luna.

PAVIA, HOLY ROMAN EMPIRE

Tuesday, July 12, 1791

It was a summer evening, somewhat cool but enveloped in a warm and welcoming atmosphere. The lights of the city of Pavia were reflected on the quiet waters of the Ticino River, creating an enchanting scene of chiaroscuro that danced gently on the surface of the river.

The Covered Bridge, an architectural jewel dating back to the 14th century, stood majestically in the heart of the city, its Gothic arches rising toward the starry sky. Built of stone, the bridge was a tangible testament to Pavia's rich history, a place where the past mixed harmoniously with the present.

The brick walls that lined the bridge were covered with flowering creepers, which gave off a delicate scent in the air.

Along the parapet, old wrought-iron lampposts illuminated the path of passersby, casting a golden glow on the faces of the people who looked out over the river.

The Ticino River flowed silently under the bridge, its slow flow lulled by the gentle murmur of the waters. A few boats moored along the banks added a touch of life to the landscape, while the lights of their lanterns danced on the surface of the water.

For the Professor and Rosina, the Covered Bridge represented a haven, a place where they could retreat from the city's noise and find a moment of peace and serenity. It was here that they had gone in search of solace, hoping to find relief from their worries and consolation in each other's embrace.

As they watched the golden reflection of the moon on the dark river, a courier approached the Professor, gave a letter to him with a solemn air. The Professor was waiting for that missive, whose unwanted content he already imagined. He took it with a trembling hand, opened it and already after the first line stopped reading, having understood that it was the message that, sooner or later, he would receive. Rosina noticed the change in his face and moved a few steps closer. "What it?" she asked in a worried voice, full of anxiety.

The Professor lifted his gaze, his eyes grave with barely concealed sadness. "It is a letter from Vienna," he said softly, "it is from the emperor himself. He has intervened to prevent our marriage."

The words fell like heavy stones between them, creating an atmosphere of bewilderment and dismay. Rosina felt her heart tighten in her chest, a sense of disbelief and despair enveloping her like a dark cloak.

The Professor laid the letter on the bridge parapet with a trembling hand as he tried to find the right words to comfort Rosina. But what could he say in the face of such a blow, such an injustice that threatened to break their love?

Looking into each other's eyes, they both realized that their lives were destined to take a different turn, marked by the imperial veto that was ending their dreams of marital bliss.

During those two years, the Professor and Rosina experienced a love affair that had flourished like a secret garden in the heart of the city of Pavia. Their meetings took place in quiet and secluded places, far from the prying eyes and gossip of society.

However, they had not reckoned with the social conventions of the time.

Pavia was part of the dominions of Austria, a big and powerful empire that stretched over much central and eastern Europe. The emperor of Austria, Leopold II, ruled this empire with a firm hand, guiding it with a conservative and authoritarian policy.

In the geopolitical context of the time, Austria faced numerous challenges and rivalries with other neighboring states, such as Prussia, revolutionary France, and the nascent Kingdom of Sardinia. These maintained complex and often conflicting relations, seeking to preserve their interests and consolidate their power in a Europe in turmoil. The politics of the time were marked by power struggles, unstable alliances, and incessant conflict, with the Emperor of Austria finding himself at the center of this intricate web of international relations. His decisions influenced not only the fate of his empire but also that of other nations and of their inhabitants.

Austria's dominance was also felt in the daily lives of its citizens, with the laws and regulations imposed by the emperor governing their lives and social relations.

Given the professor's role in Pavia academia and his direct knowledge of Emperor Leopold II, underestimating his possible intervention had been a big mistake.

The silence had grown thick between the Professor and Rosina, as the weight of the words spoken weighed on their shoulders like a boulder. The Professor had told Rosina the news of the Emperor of Austria's intervention in an atonal voice and downcast eyes, knowing that those words would change the course of their love affair. It was as if the Covered Bridge, the usual refuge of their moment's intimacy and happiness, had witnessed the silent drama of their broken hearts.

Rosina, holding her breath and her eyes moist with unshed

tears, struggled to comprehend the extent of the tragedy that was unfolding.

The Professor, though heartbroken, knew that the decision they had to make was inevitable. The rigid social conventions and the power of the Emperor of Austria left no room for their happiness. They had to separate, to protect what remained of their dignity and to avoid additional painful consequences.

In the silence pregnant with meaning, as the Ticino continued to flow under the Covered Bridge, they looked into each other's eyes with determination. "We cannot continue as before," whispered the Professor, his voice imbued with sadness and resignation. "But neither can we give up our scientific collaboration."

Rosina nodded, understanding the complexity of the situation. They had shared so much, not only moments of love but also passionate discussions and scientific discoveries that had united them in a unique way. "We have an opportunity," she added firmly, "to continue to cultivate our bond through science, through research and knowledge that has united us from the beginning."

So, in the middle of the night, under the starry sky of Pavia, they decided to preserve at least part of their connection, pledging to continue their scientific collaboration. It was a glimmer of hope at a time of great sadness, a sign that their bond would not be completely broken, despite the hardships that fate had in store for them.

IBARAKI, JAPAN

Wednesday, January 16, 2019

Luna awoke early with the gentle, steady sound of the digital alarm clock beside her bed, a gentle reminder that gently interrupted her dreams. Next to the alarm clock, on the bedside table, was a hotel brochure outlining the breakfast options available. With a sigh of satisfaction from her night's rest, Luna got up and walked over to the window to watch the morning begin to unfold. After a quick refreshing shower, she went down to the floor of the breakfast, where the air was permeated with the inviting aroma of freshly cooked rice and fresh fish. The buffet was a riot of colors and flavors, with a wide selection of traditional Japanese and international dishes. Along with the varied array of rice and fish dishes, there were also hot soups, eggs cooked in a thousand different ways, fresh salads, and a selection of seasonal fruits.

Luna served herself plentifully, savoring each mouthful calmly as she prepared for the day ahead. The soothing warmth of green tea enveloped her as she sipped slowly, enjoying the quiet and serene atmosphere of the hotel dining room.

After finishing her breakfast with a slice of traditional Japanese dessert, Luna felt invigorated and ready to face the day. With a full belly and an uplifted spirit, she exited the hotel to direct her steps toward the Choshi Kosei Library, a few hundred meters away, ready to immerse herself in the pages of knowledge that awaited her.

From the hotel lobby, he saw that the rain, which had recently begun to fall, was intensifying, turning the view into a gray curtain that obscured the view of the surrounding buildings. Next to the hotel was a Conbini, the typical Japanese convenience store that often offered immediate solutions to the needs of passersby. So, without hesitation, she spent 500 yen to buy one of those transparent umbrellas typical of Japanese cities on rainy days, hoping that at least that gesture might provide her with some shelter from the storm that was brewing.

Protected by her new umbrella, she walked the short distance to the library.

The building in front of her made a little positive impression: a mass of gray concrete, blackened by the ravages of time, lacking any ornamentation or care for style. It was as if the architecture itself reflected a sense of grayness and abandonment, accentuating her growing unease as she approached the gloomy building.

At the entrance, with an automatic gesture, she left her umbrella in the umbrella stand along with many others all identical, which made her wonder about the slim chance of getting exactly the same one back on the way out, but that realization did not seem to interest anyone: one umbrella was as good as another, and no one was interested in getting exactly the same one back with which they arrived.

Without hesitation, Luna headed for the secretary's office, determined to speak with the director. The dull sound of rain beat steadily against the windows, accompanied by gusts of wind that seemed to whisper a warning to her ear. The air was damp and cold, and the atmosphere inside the building seemed to mirror the turmoil outside.

Mr. Ito arrived after two minutes, walking briskly. He was a middle-aged man of medium build, with well-combed gray hair and thin glasses that gave him an air of wisdom. His face was marked by deep wrinkles, a sign of years of experience and dedication to the work.

Apologizing for the wait, he introduced himself with a gentle smile that contrasted with the stormy weather outside. "Good morning, you must be Kobayashi-san. Kato-san anticipated that you would come," said Mr. Ito, with his warm voice.

"Nice to meet you, Ito-san, thank you very much for your helpfulness," Luna replied with a little bow, feeling immediately reassured by Ito-san's presence.

"Kato-san asked me to show you the library's historical archives but didn't provide much detail. Can you explain more about what you are looking for? If you go through papers without a clear direction, you will never finish," said Mr. Ito, in a kind but pragmatic tone.

Luna nodded, trying to organize her thoughts. "Actually, I'm not clear either. I need documents related to the early 1800s, maybe I would start with the registry records. I'm looking for information about a Shoya from that era, I'd like to at least find his name," Luna replied, looking dubious.

Mr. Ito looked at her with understanding and a slight smile. "I understand, it's a daunting task, but let's see what we can do. Follow me, I'll show you where to start," he said, pointing in the direction with a wave of his hand.

Mr. Ito, kind and courteous, accompanied Luna down a short corridor that led to the basement of the library. Despite the dimness that enveloped the passage, Luna felt safe in the librarian's company. The walls were lined with light wood paneling that gave the hallway a cozy atmosphere despite the relative darkness.

Dim lights cast a soft glow on the polished marble floor, creating a kind of light path that invited them to explore the basement of the library. Mr. Ito graciously explained the various sections of the library as they proceeded, illuminating the vastness and diversity of resources available.

The basement, although darker than the exterior facade, was not at all frightening. Luna noticed that, despite the lack of natural light, the room was well lit by ceiling lights that diffused a warm and welcoming light. Shelves filled with books stood out neatly along the walls, offering endless possibilities for exploration and discovery. The soft sound of footsteps on the marble floor helped create an atmosphere of tranquility and concentration.

"Can I leave you here? Will you be able to find your way out when you're done?" asked Mr. Ito, stopping in front of a shelf full of dusty folders.

"Certainly. Can I consult anything I want?" re- espoused Luna with a mixture of enthusiasm and gratitude.

57

"Yes, Kato-san has vouched for you. I'm sure he'll put everything back in order," Ito said with a confident smile.

"Can I take pictures?" asked Luna, hoping to document her findings.

"Sure," Ito replied. "See you later." With a final nod of encouragement, he walked away, leaving Luna immersed in the documents.

Immersed in the library, Luna found herself enveloped in an atmosphere of mystery and history as she explored folders of documents dating back to the early 1800s. The folders, carefully preserved and delicately stacked on dark wooden shelves, seemed to hide secrets and adventures from the past.

Spending days in the archives was a joyous time for Luna. Her friends seemed skeptical when she recounted having to spend many hours indoors looking at old documents but they had no idea how archives were living places, where she could talk to people who had left her their voices when they were still alive.

With a light hand, Luna opened one of the folders and plunged into the world of 19th century Japan. She found documents that told stories of samurai and daimyo but, more importantly, administrative records that traced the daily lives of ordinary people.

Among the yellowed pages of travel diaries, Luna discovered detailed descriptions Japanese daily life, customs, and traditions of the time. In one such diaries, allegedly written by a local traveler named Takeshi Yamamoto, Luna found a vivid account of his encounter with a farming family in rural Ibaraki.

Yamamoto described with rich detail the simple but vibrant life of the peasants, from their food customs to their religious festivals. He told of the long days spent in the rice fields, under the scorching sun, and evenings spent around the fire, telling stories told by generations.

One of the most memorable passages in Yamamoto's diary concerned a traditional ceremony that had taken place in the village during his visit. He described the festive atmosphere, with lanterns lit and stalls filled with food and handcrafted souvenirs. Children played among the village streets, while adults gathered for prayers and offerings at the local shrine.

Through Yamamoto's words, Luna felt transported back in time, imagining the vivid and colored scenes of Choshi village in the 1800s. Her discovery confirmed how much research in the folders could reveal not historical facts but also the lives and emotions of the people who populated those lands centuries ago. In addition to the stories, Luna also found hand-drawn maps showing the villages and towns of the Ibaraki region, with surprisingly accurate detail for the time. Annotations in the margins of the maps offered clues to mysterious places and local legends, fueling Luna's imagination and prompting her to want to find out more.

It was the insistent rumbling of her stomach that made her feel the urgency to focus on what she was looking for instead of scattering herself in general searches. With a quick move, she took the onigiri she had providently prepared in advance and gratefully enjoyed it, recognizing the importance nourishing the body to feed the mind.

Once the sudden hunger was satisfied, she immersed herself in carefully preserved documents dating from 1800 to 1807. Armed with patience and determination, she scanned yellowed pages and faded ink for clues, names and dates that might shed light on the mystery she was trying to solve.

After a brief search, she arrived at the document she was looking for: a kind of registry book of the time. The parchment she was reading contained a list of names, social positions and dates. For most people, there was only one date, most likely the date of death, while for the Shoya, in addition to the names, two dates were listed, probably the date on which they had begun holding the position and the date of termination, which, since it was a life position, corresponded to the date of death.

She had to find the name of the country's Shoya in 1807. He began to read the names from that period: Yano 1791-1794, Mizuno 1794-1802, Kimura 1807-1819.

The period 1802-1807 was missing, the very Shoya period she

was looking for! The flag had been commandeered to the Shoya in 1807, a date that corresponded to the date of his death. Could it have been a fluke? Or had that flag angered someone enough to kill the Shoya? She was in a bind; without his name, she could find no more information about why an Italian flag had come to Japan.

She turned the parchment over to close it and noticed a small text on the back: 'Register 1807, Enpuku-Ji.' Enpuku-Ji was a small temple located a few hundred meters from the library. It had no other way, so we might as well go and visit that place as well.

On his way out, she stopped to greet Ito.

"Ito-san, I found the document I was looking for, although it wasn't much help," Luna said, trying to hide her disappointment.

"How come?" asked Ito, with an expression of sincere interest.

"I found the register at the place you suggested but the name of the Shoya was not present. The only name that was missing was from the very period of my interest," Luna explained, shaking her head.

"I'm sorry," Ito replied, in a tone of understanding. "What are you going to do now?"

"I saw a reference to a register at the Enpuku-Ji temple and was thinking of going there now. What should I expect?" asked Luna, hopeful.

"It may be interesting," Ito said. "While in this library all general documents are stored, in the temple there are archives of official communications of some significance, divided by year. Do you have a specific year to look for?"

"Yes, 1807," Luna replied, with a glimmer of hope. "Good; there are usually no more than a couple of documents for each year. You have really intrigued me. Do you mind if I accompany you? Then I can help you find the register you're looking for right away," Ito proposed enthusiastically.

"Thank you very much, Ito-san!" replied Luna, feeling a wave of gratitude.

By the time they left the library it had stopped raining and a pale sun had come out. Because of this, Luna would only realize in the evening that she had completely forgotten her new umbrella, which then, as expected, would become someone else's.

Enpuku-Ji was a charming Buddhist temple surrounded by lush forests and a serene atmosphere. Built about 1,200 years earlier, one of its highlights was its beautiful main building, with traditional Japanese architecture that blended harmoniously with the surrounding landscape. Luna was fascinated by the intricate details of the wooden structures and the pitched roofs that lent a sense of sacredness and grandeur to the place.

Mr. Ito walked determinedly toward a small building with the keys. Inside was a large filing cabinet with the various drawers identified by the year of reference.

"This is where the documents of this region are stored," Ito explained. "Documents of important historical value are obviously in museums, but even here one occasionally finds some surprises; one would have to have a lot of time to read everything, even considering that much of the contents are absolutely indecipherable. Please do yourself the honor of opening the 1807 drawer!"

Luna, excited, opened the drawer. There were several pergamene, but her enthusiasm quickly waned as she opened and read them. The text was difficult to read, using archaic characters that even she struggled to interpret but eventually, and Ito's help, she recognized in the texts just some confused poems, probably written by children

人の夢
宀の下に眠る
宀に星

("People's dreams / They sleep under the roof / Stars under the roof") and texts written perhaps in jest:

寺は再び谷疑者の豕を探した

("The temple again searched for the suspect's pig of the valley.")

"From your expression," Ito said, "I guess you weren't looking for poems written by children."

"No, definitely not," Luna replied in a low voice.

"As I told you, documents of some relevance are all in museums, so I'm sorry I couldn't help you."

"Ito-san, it helped me so much, regardless of the outcome," Luna said. "If you don't mind, I'll still take some pictures of these papers, maybe I'll find a way to keep them in my research."

"Go ahead," Ito replied.

By now it was late to return to Tokyo, so she headed back to the hotel from the night before and, walking sadly under a now starry sky, telephoned Gabriele.

TOKYO, JAPAN

Saturday, March 26, 2016

Hanami. How many times had he heard that word repeated since he found out he was moving to Japan? Cherry blossom, the most sacred time of the Japanese year. He had high expectations and feared he would be disappointed. He had seen cherry blossom parks before, so what could be different?

His apartment overlooked Meiji Dori. Generally, streets in Tokyo did not have names (perhaps there were not enough names to assign to all those streets and roads); exceptions were the main thoroughfares including, indeed, Meiji Dori, which connected the Minato and Shibuya quarters. The avenue was lined with cherry trees that, green when he arrived, had shed their leaves in November and, the day before, had begun to show small buds.

He left the house around 9 a.m. to go to Chokokro's for breakfast, which for the past week had resumed selling the white chocolate croissants that drove him crazy.

As soon as he walked out of the building's front door, he was left speechless. How could this be the same place seen only a few hours earlier? The branches had exploded with pink petals.

He walked over to a flower and stared at it closely, like a child looking at a ladybug resting on his hand.

No, the flower was not pink, it was definitely white but with very faint pink streaks that from a distance gave the elegant effect for which this phenomenon was world-famous. And that was precisely the difference with the cherry blossoms he was used to. The flowers he knew were pink, an almost mundane color. He had never seen anything like it.

He did not head to Chokokro but strolled along Meiji Dori looking around as if it were the first time he walked in that place. He arrived at the center of the Hiroo district and headed almost unintentionally toward Arisugawa Park. On the way he picked up a croissant and a take-away cappuccino at a Lavazza Cafe and sat down to have breakfast on a park bench. There were not many cherry trees in the park, but wind-blown petals came and settled on the placid waters of the pond, confounding the Koi carp swimming in it. Was this the Zen that was talked about so much? He did not know, and he did not care to give it a definition; he was just enjoying the moment.

Two hours later he was in Yoyogi park, the green oasis in the heart of Tokyo. With its ponds, tree-lined avenues, spacious parks, sports areas, and shrines (the Meiji shrine above all), it was the perfect place for a picnic with friends under the blossoming cherry trees.

Everyone was there: Takeshi, Hiro, Marta, Davide, Marco and Hiah (who said nothing but always arrived together and left together), and Luna. Kiyoshi, a former professor of Luna who was only a few years older than them, had now been added to the group for a few weeks.

They were not often seen together, and everyone news to tell.

Takeshi recounted that his store had reached its budget for the year only the evening of the previous day, at the very last moment: in Japan the fiscal year ends at the end of March, so that was the time for company budgets. Takeshi made everyone smile when he recounted that it was 2 Man (about 200 dollars) short of reaching the year's turnover target when a lady, just at the edge of closing time, had come in to buy a bag but had chosen a 1.6 Man bag! The employee bonus was formally at risk; therefore, it had been he himself to purchase, at the very last moment, a 0.4 Man belt; budget reached and applause from all colleagues. Hiro and Marta updated the group on the status of their exams, Kiyoshi announced that he had just changed jobs and in two weeks would become deputy director of a library near Yokohama.

During the discussion, they had eaten lunch with what they had brought from home or had purchased at local Conbini. Almost everyone had brought onigiri, rice balls covered seaweed. That was the main snack of any Japanese person, somewhat like a pizzetta or focaccia might be in Italy.

Gabriele was fickle about that, too; he didn't like the salty taste of seaweed, so he had fallen back on a Tonkatsu sandwich, a Japanese culinary delight consisting of a savory pork cutlet enclosed between two slices of soft bread. Although eating a cold cutlet was not exactly his preference, the addition of the barbecue sauce gave the sandwich an intriguing flavor that made it a worthy choice.

After lunch, he bought at a vending machine a can of hot latte. Yes, hot latte in a can. That was a transgression that none of his acquaintances in Italy would ever have to discover. In Japan he could share this habit without too much thought but, in Italy, to confess such a sin was to attract the scorn of any citizen. It was like admitting preferring wine in cartons to Chianti or frozen pizza to pizza from a wood-fired oven. He had to hide from himself the pleasure he took in such an unorthodox beverage, as if to safeguard his Italic honor and reputation as a lover of authentic coffee.

In winter, bringing a can of hot coffee to the office was a pleasant cuddle against the cold, while in summer, fresh coffee was a refreshing break. It was the distributors who decided when the temperature should change and everyone had to adapt, thus marking the transition between hot and cold seasons. Ironic how it was a machine that dictated the pace of the seasons, making his little ritual even more of a guilty secret to be jealously guarded.

As he drank his coffee, he noticed that Marco's hand was resting on Hiah's knee. Marco didn't tell it all to him. He had to find him alone for a moment and be told. Without knowing why, he turned his gaze toward Luna, who had her face turned upward and, with her eyes closed, was enjoying a warm breeze. Her face was more shining than ever.

He pulled out a chocolate from his backpack and asked Luna if she would like one.

She replied, "Daijoubu."

Daijoubu. The word encapsulated the very essence of Japanese language, an archetype of its ambiguous delicacy of expression, reason why neither a dictionary nor an automatic translator could ever replace direct study of that language.

In the dictionary, Daijoubu literally meant "okay," but after the time spent in Japan and the many misunderstandings experienced, Gabriele understood that Luna did not desire the chocolate at all, even though she would have used the exact same word to accept it.

The secret lay in the tone: pronounced firmly, Daijoubu meant "all right!"; said in a subdued, almost apologetic tone, and perhaps accompanied by a slight horizontal movement of the hand, it meant "I'm fine, so I don't need it."

A similar situation often occurred at work when a Japanese person used the word "Muzukashii" literally: "difficult."

Question, "Dear customer X, can you accept this product modification?" Answer: "Muzukashii." The customer did not mean it was "difficult" to accept the modification; it meant that there was no chance. It was a definitive "no" with no possibility of discussion, however, the direct "no" counted as an insult, so it could never be used.

Gabriele's Japanese colleagues were unaware of this cultural misalignment and, in the minutes for Italy, communicated that it was "difficult" for customer X to accept the change. Italian managers interpreted this "difficult" as a still open possibility and insisted, creating an endless cycle of requests and refusals.

In the end, Gabriele had decided to revise all the minutes that crossed continents, replacing each "difficult" with a firm "no."

With a sigh of resignation, he wondered how many more cultural nuances he was missing, then put the chocolate back in his backpack.

BERGAMO, ITALY

Wednesday, January 16, 2019

At lunchtime, Gabriele received Luna's phone call. "Hello Gabriele, am I disturbing you?"

"Absolutely not, I'm on my lunch break." Hearing Luna's voice gave him the same emotions as before.

"How are you? Seen the flag?"

"Yes, you are right, it is indeed an Italian flag. But at that time Northern Italy was under French rule and on the back it says Paris, so it must have something to do with France. Definitely not with Japan..."

"This is where I found it, though. What year could it be?" asked Luna.

"Definitely after 1796, so the period in theory would be the correct one. There must be something else written on the back. I tried to use graphics processing software here in the office this morning but all the licenses are in use, maybe I will be able to do it tomorrow. With this software I'll probably be able to read what's written before the word Paris."

"Thanks for the help, Gabriele!" said Luna. "Although probably we are at a standstill." Luna told him about her visit to Choshi Library and Enpuku-Ji Temple, reciting one of the poems she had memorized.

Gabriele said nothing. "Gabriele, can you hear me?" asked Luna.

"Yes, I hear you," he replied in a neutral tone.

Luna was hurt; he seemed indifferent. Perhaps he was having thoughts about work and she was disturbing him.

"Okay, I hear you busy, 'll catch up another time," and she prepared to end the conversation.

"No! Wait a minute, I was thinking," exclaimed Gabriele. "Can you tell me the first poem and the beginning of the text again?"

Luna was confused "Certainly: the poem says, 'People's dreams / Sleep under the roof / Stars under the roof,' and the text starts with 'The temple has again sought the pig of the valley suspect.'

Does that ring a bell?"

Gabriele was silent ten seconds, an eternity during a phone call, then said, "The poem repeats the word 'roof' quite forcibly and, in the text, the strangest word is 'pig.' I remember a Japanese class in which the instructor explained to me that 'roof' and 'pig' are the radicals of 'house.'" Another five seconds of silence: "Surely this is not a code text, of which poems are the key?"

Now it was Luna who remained silent, perhaps a whole minute, her mind whirling. 'Roof' 宀 plus 'pig' 豕 equals 'house' 家. Then? Another out-of-context word was 'valley,' and the word 'roof' was repeated: 'roof' 宀 plus 'valley' 谷 equals 'container' 容 but, most importantly, 谷疑者 'the suspect of the valley' became 容疑者 'the suspect of a crime. She tried with the first line of the poem and the first word of the text: 'person' 人 plus 'temple' 寺 equals 侍 which meant... It was not possible... It meant 'Samurai'!

"Luna? Are you there?"

"Gabriele you are a genius!" shouted Luna. "The first sentence of the text is not 'The temple again searched the pig of the suspect of the valley' but 'the samurai searched again at the home of the suspect'! This is a coded record of the questioning that the samurai did to the shoya who had found the flag! Gabriele, I have to go, I'll call you as soon as I've translated the whole text."

"All right, Luna, just try to..." said Gabriele but Luna did not hear him, she had already ended the call. She would surely be up all night.

SEOUL, KOREA

Monday, March 28, 2016

Gabriele's career path in Japan extended as far as Korea. This was not dictated by a specific business strategy but, rather, by a historical tradition.

Automitalia had entered the Far East as early as the 1980s, starting in Japan and establishing an initial small technical and sales team. Once it had achieved major successes in Japan, the group had begun to look outward and establish contacts with potential customers in the area, which at the time included exclusively Korean automakers.

Although the business had begun to move gradually, its relevance was still limited. Therefore, one of Gabriele's goals was to enhance the company's presence in that market as well.

In his first six months in Japan, he had visited Korea often and an opportunity was finally emerging. At this stage he knew he had to be patient, despite the pressure from the headquarters to bring results right away. Automitalia had an outstanding product and reputation, his job should have been simple, but he had realized early on that in Asia it was necessary to be patient, to be available to customers, to visit them, to focus on technique and quality instead of branding, to listen to them, and to be ready in time of need. He felt that moment was approaching, so he had to visit the customer as often as possible.

He was excited about the possibility: the business under discussion would bring Korea's business volume almost on par with Japan's but, on a personal level, he was not happy. Getting from Japan to Korea was not pleasant: he left a clear blue sky and landed with gray, and although he was at the same latitude as Tokyo, was ten degrees lower. He could not remember ever seeing a clear blue sky in Seoul. He didn't like the way the taxi drivers drove, who were constantly braking and accelerating, he didn't like the long checks at the airport, he didn' like the way many Koreans talked by touching people, he didn't like the smell of bibimbap, a traditional Korean dish that consisted of a bowl of rice mixed with various vegetables, spinach, soybean sprouts, zucchini, carrots and mushrooms, meat (usually marinated beef or ground beef) and egg, all mixed with fermented chili sauce (go- chujang) or soy sauce. Instead, he loved gogi-gui, a grilled meat dish that he liked to wrap in lettuce leaves along with garlic cloves. He tried to enjoy it as often as possible by frequenting restaurants that specialized in that delicacy. However, ordering that kind of dish was not always easy, so he could satisfy this craving only when he was in company. The only advantage of Seoul was that, being further west within the same time zone, sunset was about an hour later than in Tokyo.

That morning, sitting down to breakfast in the hotel, he was consuming up a sumptuous meal: eggs and bacon, cappuccino, croissants, milk and cereal. At home, he would never have imagined enjoying such a variety of delicacies upon waking up, but it was a feeling common to everyone he had talked to. There seemed to be an irrepressible craving for food in hotel restaurants, even among those who were usually satisfied with a simple coffee for breakfast.

By the second slice of bacon, he began to realize that just as he did not love Korea, Korea did not love him.

The pain began as a cramp in my right side that soon took the entire lower abdomen.

In Korea he was helped by an agent, Mr. Kim (not that saying Mr. Kim helped identify anyone in Korea, since ninety percent of the people were named Kim or Jeong), who, if not endowed with the highest managerial spirit, was among the friendliest and most helpful people he had ever met. Now that he thought about it, he also liked Mr. Kim from Korea. He was therefore happy to see him enter the hotel lobby just as he was slumping in his chair.

A few minutes later he was in the emergency room. The first question, almost ritual, concerned the coverage capacity of his credit card. Once he had confirmation that the bill would be paid, a quick X-ray confirmed the suspicion: kidney stone. The meeting with the client was postponed until the next day; Mr.

Kim would handle it without him, was no big deal. Now he had to concentrate on effective painkillers and how to get to Japan as soon as possible.

Here, too, Mr. Kim demonstrated all his helpfulness and effectiveness: discharged from the hospital stuffed with painkillers, he accompanied him to the airport in Gimpo after checking the availability of a seat on the twelve o'clock flight. The trip to Japan proved to be one of the most arduous experiences of his life: only two hours but with the constant fear that the effects of the painkillers would wear off, leaving him in pain in a plane with no escape route. Fortunately, the painkillers did their job landing at Haneda Airport. As soon as he stepped off the plane, however, the pain began to intensify again; the painkillers had worn off but he now felt safe.

Fifteen minutes by cab later, he entered the emergency room of one of Tokyo's major hospitals, realizing, amid atrocious pains, that hallucinations had begun to haunt him. Gabriele thought that visions could be strange and surprising, often showing what we basically hope to see in reality. It was as if, for a moment, the brain decided to play and allowed a glimpse of the most hidden desires. In these moments, it almost seemed as if he could touch dreams that usually seem unattainable, for example, he seemed to see Luna sitting in the waiting room running up to him and hugging him.

By the time he woke up, about four hours later, it was evening. He had a vague memory of entering the hospital, Luna waiting for him. He slowly opened his eyes and saw the room he was in, illuminated by a soft light. Now he felt no more pain, only a great hunger.

"Gabriele, how do you feel?" he heard whispering.

"Luna? What are you doing here?" he asked, surprised to see her.

"Tell me how you feel and then let's talk about something else," she replied, concerned.

"Now I have no pain, just a great hunger," Gabriele said, trying to get his bearings. "How did you know I was here?"

"Baka desu! You texted me from the cab!"

A shiver came down Gabriele's spine. Yes, he had a vague recollection of writing a message... Oh no... He also remembered the message: 'Luna, I'm going to the hospital Aiku, I'm in a lot of pain, I miss you.'

Oh no, oh no, oh no... In his youth he had written late-night drunken texts that he regretted a moment later but this crossed that line and did not even have the excuse of alcohol. Perhaps he could blame it on the painkillers.

He put his hand over his eyes, "Hazukashii..." what a shame...

Luna smiled embarrassedly. "I've been worried, I ran here as soon as I could."

"But how did you get there before me? From the time I texted you to the time I saw you the emergency room, it must have been fifteen minutes at most!" asked Gabriele.

"No... When I arrived you had been sleeping for a couple of hours in this room. I wasn't in the emergency room. Did you even have a hallucination where you saw me?" asked Luna winking.

"Hazukashii..." Enough, on pain medication he would never speak again.

Now, however, he had to update the list of positive points Korea: to business opportunities, the gogi-gui, the sunset time, the very friendly people, he had to add the foundation for the birth of the relationship between him and Luna.

BERGAMO, ITALY

Wednesday, January 16, 2019

On the phone Luna had sounded very agitated, she was putting a lot of effort into that research, she had to help as soon as possible.

Looking at the internal resource schedule, he had seen that the licenses for the graphics processing software would become free two days later but he knew that if he waited until late, sooner or later he would be able to use a license without having to make reservations.

So indeed it happened, around 7:45 p.m. He uploaded the image he had received to his cell phone and started background removal routine. He repeated the task several times until he got a result that he found acceptable.

The writing was fading more and more to the left but the letters he could read were: '...rianna Paris.' Before that there might have been a couple of letters. It took him little time to interpret the missing word as 'Marianne', the famous symbol of the French Revolution.

With this information he no longer needed to stay in the office and headed home.

During the short drive he thought about what he had found, and the association between the French Marianne and Paris became quite obvious to him.

He arrived home, put water on the stove for the usual pasta with tomato sauce, turned on the PC, opened a search engine, typed in 'Marianne Paris,' and read what he already knew:

The term "Marianne" as a symbol of the French Republic has historical roots dating back to the French Revolution of 1789 and is often personified as a female figure embodies republican values.

The name "Marianne" may have come from a combination of the names "Marie" and "Anne," which were common names in France that period. The connection between the name "Marianne" and the symbolic representation of the Republic became more evident during

the 19th century.'
Thus, another connection between the time period, at the turn of the late 18th and early 19th centuries, and the geopolitical situation, namely the entry of France into northwestern Italy, was evident.

During dinner he continued to wonder how he could have gotten that object to Japan. He tried to imagine a possible route, considering that travel from Italy to Japan took a long time due to limited transportation options and logistical difficulties at the time. Journeys were made by sea, and the time required depended on various factors, including sea routes, weather conditions, and the naval technology available at the time.

A journey from Italy to Japan in the 1800s could have involved two possible routes: one going east and one going west.

However, the departure would probably have been from Genoa, a major seafaring city of the time. The ship would have plied the waters of the Mediterranean Sea, sailing along the northern coast of Africa until it reached the Strait of Gibraltar, the gateway to the Atlantic Ocean.

After crossing the Strait of Gibraltar, one could continue westward, and the voyage continued into the Atlantic Ocean, pointing south along the west coast of Africa. This part of the voyage could be particularly difficult because of storms and strong currents. The ship would call at some African port to supplies and repair any damage.

Having reached the western end of the African continent, the ship would continue westward, crossing the Atlantic to the South American coast, perhaps stopping in Rio de Janeiro or Montevideo for additional supplies and to prepare for the difficult Cape Horn crossing.

Upon reaching the southern tip of South America, the ship would round Cape Horn, known for its dangerous waters with violent winds and high waves that tested the endurance of sailors and boats. This was one of the most treacherous stretches of the voyage, often marked by storms and severe weather.

Once past Cape Horn, the ship would enter the Pacific Ocean.

Navigation would continue along the western coast of South America, with possible stops at ports such as Valparaíso in Chile for supplies and repairs.

After leaving the South American coast, the ship would head northwest across the vastness of the Pacific Ocean. The Galápagos Islands could be a further stop for supplies. The Pacific crossing was long and monotonous, with the risk of illness and food deficiencies always lurking.

Finally, the ship would have reached the Asian coast, probably passing between the islands of the Philippines, and then heading north through the South China Sea and Taiwan Strait. Following the Chinese coast, the ship would have entered the Sea of Japan.

Alternatively, an eastward route could have been taken. Arriving at the Cape of Good Hope, at the southern end of Africa, the ship would have faced the dangerous and often stormy waters of that region. Once past the Cape, the ship would have continued northeast along the east coast of Africa, stopping at strategic ports such as Durban or Mombasa, and then continuing to Indian Ocean.

Crossing the Indian Ocean, the ship could have called at the Seychelles Islands or Mauritius for an additional stop. The voyage would then continue eastward, crossing the equator and navigating tropical waters.

At this point, the route would have veered northeast, routing into the South China Sea. Here the ship would likely have called at important ports such as Singapore or Hong Kong, two trading hubs for trade with the Far East.

Finally, the ship would enter the Sea of Japan and head for one of Japan's major ports, such as Nagasaki or Yokohama.

In general, a trip from Italy to Japan in the early 1800s would have taken several months, if not years. Unless, of course, one had a vessel dedicated to that journey. In that case, perhaps a couple of months would have been sufficient.

Added to this was the politics of Japan at that time.

The first Europeans to arrive in Japan were the Portuguese, in 1543. Three Portuguese castaways are said to have been the first Europeans to touch Japanese soil on Tanegashima Island, located south of Kyushu. These castaways taught the Japanese the use of firearms, particularly the arquebus.

Later, in 1549, the Spanish Jesuit missionary Francis Xavier arrived in Japan, bringing the Catholic religion with him. The European presence in Japan grew further with the arrival of Portuguese and Spanish traders, Christian missionaries and other individuals from different parts of Europe.

However, over time, Japanese authorities became increasingly concerned about the growing influence of Christianity and the introduction of firearms. In 1614, the Japanese government of the Tokugawa shogunate issued an edict banning Christianity and banning foreign missionaries from the country. This led to a period of isolation of the Japanese empire, known as Sakoku, which lasted until 1853. During this long period of closure, Japan maintained a policy of almost total isolation from outside influences, severely limiting commercial and diplomatic contacts with other nations.

The situation changed dramatically in July 1853, when Commodore Matthew Perry of the U.S. Navy arrived in Japanese waters with a fleet of warships, known as the 'Black Ships' because of their dark hulls. Perry had been commissioned by President Millard Fillmore to negotiate the opening of Japanese ports to international trade and to secure better conditions for shipwrecked sailors.

Perry arrived in Edo Bay, the future Tokyo, with four ships: the USS Mississippi, the USS Plymouth, the USS Saratoga, and the USS Susquehanna. The impressive and intimate presence of the Black Ships forced Japan to seriously consider American requests. Perry delivered a letter from President Fillmore to the Japanese government, requesting the opening of ports for trade and assistance to shipwrecked sailors.

After a year of negotiations and further show of force by Perry, Japan agreed to sign the Treaty of Kanagawa on March 31, 1854. This treaty marked the end of the Sakoku and the beginning of a new era of openness and modernization for Japan. Under the treaty, ports of Shimoda and Hakodate were opened to American ships, an American consul was established in Japan, and better conditions were guaranteed for shipwrecked sailors.

Perry's arrival and the signing of the Treaty of Kanagawa had a profound and lasting impact on Japan. The end of isolation forced the country to confront foreign powers and triggered a series of internal reforms that culminated in the fall of the Shogunate and the Meiji Restoration of 1868. This period saw Japan rapidly transform from an isolated feudal society into a modern industrial power capable of competing on the world stage.

However, Gabriele recalled reading that even before Commodore Perry's arrival there were some cases of contact between the United States and Japan but they were not of great scope or regularity. For example, he recalled the case of the Lady Washington, commanded by John Kendrick, which had not landed but came very close to the shores of Japan around 1800 and the case of the crew of the U.S. fishing ship Morrison commanded by Charles W. King, which wrecked on the Japanese coast in 1837. The crew were treated with suspicion and taken to Nagasaki, where they were briefly detained.

In short, nothing to help imagine how the Italian flag had arrived in Japan.

He went to bed and closed his eyes thinking of brigs, galleons, flags, Napoleonic battles, Marianne... Marianne!!!

He opened his eyes wide, got out of bed and rushed to the computer.

CHOSHI, JAPAN

Thursday, January 17, 2019

Luna was speechless, her vision was blurred, and her head was spinning. It was 11 a.m., she had not slept, was well past the hotel checkout time, had not had dinner, and had not had breakfast. But this was not the cause of her dizziness.

With the code identified by Gabriele, she had translated the text that now showed itself clearly to her in all its meaning and all its implications.

She had in front of her a document that changed the history of Japan, and perhaps not only.

She reread it for the umpteenth time: '*The samurai searched again at the home of the suspect, the Shoya of Choshi, and found a piece of cloth in pink, white, and blue tones, with inscriptions in an unknown alphabet. This constitutes tangible evidence of the contacts Shoya had had with the barbarians who landed on February 22 of the third year of the Kyōwa era. is evident how Shoya tried to conceal this encounter. During the interrogation that led to his death, he confessed to having had an encounter with a red-haired barbarian woman who came ashore in an unusual, small, round boat without oars or sails and then fled to the sea. We also subjected Shoya's relatives and people close to him to interrogatories using the same methods, all of which ended in their deaths. Almost all confirmed his words without adding anything else; the only exceptions were a cousin who kept pleading to return to the cave, another cousin who mentioned a rare woman, and a brother who mentioned a hiding place to south. None of these people added anything else, and the suspicion is that they were delirious: the physical and mental condition of the people in that moment, one step away from death, are probably the cause of their confusion. No further information has been obtained. We humbly beg forgiveness for the delay in sending this message and urge that the information be forwarded to the U.S. government.*'

She struggled to think rationally, but there could be no doubt.

'February 22 of the third year of the Kyōwa era,' 'round boat,' 'red-haired barbarian woman.' That was a bedtime story that all children heard; it was not a true story. It was as if she had just read a historical account of Cinderella losing the crystal slipper while escaping from the prince's castle. But it had to be: it was the Utsuro Bune. The Italian flag had been brought to Japan by an Italian woman. The princess of the Utsuro Bune was an Italian woman!

She had been so shocked to find a reference to the Utsuro Bune that she had almost left out perhaps the most astonishing historical fact: 'we urge that the information be forwarded to the U.S. government.' It is 1807. There is no relationship between the Japanese government and foreign nations. At least not officially since, evidently, relationships existed and, from the tone used, those who had written that report were very concerned that the delay might irritate the American government.

Right, who could have been the author of that text? The signature, 作武義範, could have been interpreted in various ways, but as far as the surname 作武 was concerned, was no doubt: Satake, the very family of the region's rulers of the time. That letter had to have been written by the govern himself! And, from the tone, it must have been addressed to his superior. Thanks to his research on the subject, Luna could already guess the answer to that question: the recipient of that letter was Tokugawa Narinobu, a member of the Tokugawa clan, the shogun family that had ruled Japan for over a century and would remain in power for at least another fifty years.

Also to put his thoughts in order, she transcribed what she had discovered: on February 22, 1803, a strange boat arrives in Japan, bringing with it a red-haired woman who delivers an Italian flag to the village Shoya, who keeps the information secret from the Satake clan government, whose territory is affected by the arrival of the mysterious vessel. The Satake family, informed of this encounter, conducts an investigation that lasts at least four years and, in 1807, finds the flag hidden in the Shoya's house. During questioning, the Shoya claims that the woman has escaped, but the truth remains uncertain. Both he and his family are subjected to torture until death, the date of which coincides perfectly with the documents found in Choshi's library. The information finally reaches a Tokugawa family member, who is instructed to communicate it to the U.S. government, evidently interested in the arrival of that vessel in Japan.

She could no longer keep the information only to herself. She had to share her thoughts with someone who could help her handle the burden of discovery. Fortunately, of experienced and knowledgeable people she knew enough, she just had to choose who to turn to first: Kato-san, her boss; Kiyoshi-san, her former professor at Ibaraki; or Ito- san, Choshi's librarian?

JAPAN

Thursday, January 17, 2019

"The girl is smart," he thought, sitting in his reupholstered leather chair, shaped by years of use.

She had just phoned him to update him on developments. Not that he needed to: he had been keeping a close eye on her.

The girl had found the flag but getting to the minute of Shoya's interrogation and, more importantly, being able to interpret it was not so trivial. They had deciphered the text already for a hundred years but there they had stopped. No step forward from that moment. He would have continued to observe her. He would have let her continue: a view from outside his clan could have brought the results they had been waiting for more than two centuries. Would he be the one to solve the mystery and restore dignity to his family? He had to be careful, however; he could not risk being overtaken. On the phone he had verified that she had not given this information to anyone else, and that had been a stroke of luck. Now he had to get closer to her.

And stop her, by any means, if she overtook him.

BERGAMO, ITALY

Thursday, January 17, 2019

Gabriele ran to the PC and, while waiting for it to turn on, kept repeating to himself the question that had pushed him out of bed: the name written on the flag was 'Marianna', not 'Marianne'! He sat down at his desk, opened the Google page, typed in 'Marianna Paris' and widened his eyes: *'Alessandro Volta is 43 years old when on stage he first sees Marianna Paris, a young, talented, beautiful red-haired Roman stage actress and singer...'*

PAVIA, HOLY ROMAN EMPIRE

Saturday, November 22, 1794

Marianna was reading the newspaper. She had long since shrunk from that situation, but seeing the news of Alessandro's marriage still hurt her. In any case, she had more important things to think about that day as well, so she went back to work. Two years had passed since they had implemented the first working pile together. Alessandro still did not feel like publishing the results, so he had to pretend that he was really interested in disputes with the other great scientists of the time, Luigi Galvani, a professor at the University Bologna. Galvani in an experiment had concluded that the muscles of animals were traversed by an 'electrical fluid' which, when touched with metallic material, made them contract.

Alessandro's and Marianna's studies were already ahead of their time, so they already had a good understanding of electrical phenomena but had not yet decided to expose themselves. However, Alessandro could not resist disputing those affirmations that he already knew to be false and thus began a controversy with Galvani in which he explained that it was the diversity of metals that generated the electricity that contracted the muscle, not a strange fluid present in the animal.

"Why don't you want to tell the world about our invention?" asked Marianna.

"It wouldn't be to the world, it would be to the emperor of Austria, the one who obstructed our marriage. I don't want to give this invention to Austria. I will communicate it when the time is ripe, perhaps when France chases away the Austrians from Italy," Alessandro replied.

"And will the French be better than the Austrians?"

"At least their revolutionary ideals seem noble."

Since 1792, that is, since the first working battery, they had made further remarkable progress, the most important of which was completely by accident. During an experiment, they had noticed that a compass, resting on the table near a cable deviated from north when current passed through it.

They then prepared a new experiment in which they placed a magnet bound in the center with a nail, thus allowing it to rotate. Then they had run several electrical wires around the magnet and connected them to their stack. Immediately the magnet began to rotate. They added a second stack in series with the first, and the magnet rotated at higher speed.

This created extraordinary opportunities. Not only did they have controlled electricity but also an extraordinary way to use it!

That morning Marianna was in the lab in front of their latest invention: they had built a cylinder fifty centimeters in diameter and one meter long, completely covered with magnets. They had tied it to a horizontal axis resting on trestles so that it could rotate. Outside, in a structure attached to the ground, copper cables entirely surrounded the cylinder, called a rotor. They had then set up the connection to the most powerful batteries they had but had not yet tested this system because they wanted to do the final safety checks.

For Marianna, however, it was a very bad day as her former lover was getting married. He was practically obliged to do so by an emperor, she did not hold it against him personally, however, she had decided that she would also 'betray' him. She therefore turned on the car.

The rotor began to rotate, slowly at first then, once overcame the initial inertia, faster and faster. The structure seemed to hold. When the rotor reached a stable speed, Marianna operated the system that generated an increase in potential, and the speed of the rotor increased. She reduced the potential and, as expected, the speed decreased. She was in full control of the system! She couldn't wait to tell Alessandro! She thought of her man in the arms of another woman, and the joy at the result of the experiment vanished.

OMIYA, JAPAN

Thursday, January 17, 2019

Luna was exhausted, having missed dinner, breakfast and even sleep. The accumulated fatigue weighed heavy on her shoulders and she knew she needed to rest. To regain her strength and some comfort, she decided to go to her mother and sister's house for dinner, even though she was already two days behind her original schedule. She felt that a hot meal and family company would be the perfect remedy for her fatigued state.

From Choshi to Omiya, Luna faced a train ride of more than three hours but, fortunately, only one change was necessary. She decided to make this last effort, knowing that at the end of the journey she would be welcomed and pampered, finding shelter and safety at her mother and sister's home. The train proceeded slowly, and as it approached Tokyo, it began to fill with commuters hurrying to their destinations at rush hour. Despite the increasing crowding, Luna had managed to find a seat, where she remained absorbed in her thoughts. Her mind wandered among images of waving flags, samurai in armor, and mysterious ships that sailed the distant seas.

Suddenly it occurred to her that she had not updated Gabriele and he had also not been in touch.

Of course, she would not even consider the idea of making a phone call from the train as it would violate the most sacred of the Japanese etiquette rules, so she texted him, "Gabriele, how are you? I found out something very interesting. I'm on the train now, I'll call you as soon as I get off."

She waited a moment but did not see the familiar icon of 'v' appear next to the message, a sign of successful sending. She waited a few more seconds but nothing.

Then she remembered: after alerting Emi that she was coming to visit, Luna had put her cell phone on airplane mode to give herself an hour's rest at the hotel before taking the train. Only now did she realize that she had forgotten to reactivate the connection! She immediately deactivated airplane mode and her cell phone filled with notifications: anxious messages from Gabriele urging her to call him. "Luna, call me as soon as you can," "I found out something, call me right back," "I'm trying to contact you, I'm getting worried, where are you?"

Looking around nervously, Luna felt the weight of Japanese etiquette preventing her from making a call on the train. She checked the time remaining before the next stop: only seven minutes to Higata. Just her cell phone vibrated again; Gabriele was calling, having evidently seen that she was back online. But he could not answer. Holding the phone tightly in her hand, she counted the seconds until the stop.

'Tsugiwa Higata desu, odeguchiwa migi gawa desu.'

The train announcement signaled that it was about to stop and that the doors would open on the right side. As soon as the train slowed down enough, Luna took the opportunity to initiate the call. Gabriele answered just as the train doors opened, finally allowing her to speak without infringing the polite norms of the place.

"Gabriele, I was going to..."

"Luna!" interrupted her Gabriele. "The flag bears the name of Marianna Paris, mistress of Alessandro Volta!"

Luna was silent for a moment, then said with what little breath she had in her throat, "Volta, the inventor of the pile?"

"Exactly!"

Even before the phone call, Luna's mind was in the grip of the confusion, and the new information initially seemed only to complicate things further. However, after a few moments of reflection, the details began connecting like the pieces of a puzzle. In the early 19th century, an unusual sail-less vessel had landed in Japan carrying a red-haired Western woman carrying an Italian flag. At that point, it was not so strange to think that the woman might have ties to one of the most eminent scientists of her time, given the era of great discovery and exploration.

The time had come to share her findings. In a voice that was calm but full of excitement, Luna summarized to Gabriele what she had learned from the interrogation report, which not only confirmed the historical existence of the Utsuro Bune but also opened up intriguing new perspectives on the stories and mysteries related to that era, particularly Japan's foreign policy.

"I have never heard of the Utsuro Bune, what is it about?" asked Gabriele.

"It is a legend, or at least it was until yesterday, reported in various historical sources about a strange boat that arrived in Japan in 1803. A red-haired foreign woman disembarked from this vessel and departed shortly thereafter. Given the strangeness of the situation, especially relative to a craft without sails or oars, it is often considered by ufologists as one of the earliest historical pieces of evidence of contact with an extraterrestrial life," Luna explained.

"You said the woman had red hair? Like Marianna?"

"Exactly..."

"Okay," Gabriele said, "let's assume that we have found real information and then..."

Luna interrupted Gabriele with a tone of defiance, "Why shouldn't they be real?"

Gabriele replied, adopting a didactic tone: "For Occam's Razor: a philosophical principle that suggests that among several explanations for a phenomenon, the simplest one that requires the least number of hypotheses should be preferred. This principle helps to discard the most complex and unuseful explanations."

Luna became enraged, the frustration evident in her voice. "Gabriele, don't upset me now, that I'm already tense enough," she said all in one breath. "First, I am majoring in literature, so spare me the lectures on Occam's Razor; second, I have never seen any practical application for this principle. It may be fine for some philosophical speculation, but not for anything else. In any case, I came down to this remote station especially to call you, and if it's to talk about Occam, we may as well close here and talk again another time." Without waiting for a reply, she hung up abruptly.

On the train, as the scenery whizzed by outside the window, Luna reflected on her behavior and, with a hint of self-analysis, admitted to herself that perhaps Gabriele was right. Her reaction had been so intense because she was living the dream of every scholar and history enthusiast: she was immersed in an adventure that seemed straight out of a book, and the idea of having to question the reality of that experience troubled her deeply. She did not want that dream to be interrupted.

She concentrated to formulate an alternative scenario based on the hard facts available to him: a mysterious ship had arrived on the west coast of Japan in 1803 and, inside, an Italian flag had been found with the name of a relatively well-known European personage written on it. was no doubt about this detail, since Gabriele had verified the authenticity of the flag and immediately recognized the name after a quick online search.

Applying 'Gabriele's razor's,' the most plausible hypothesis was that that piece of cloth had simply happened to be on a boat that, for unknown reasons, ended up in Japan. Although this prospect reduced the importance of the direct connection Italy, Luna could not ignore the significant discovery: a document that mentioned the Utsuro Bune. The latter discovery left little room for doubt and offered a new and historically relevant line inquiry.

The next day she would have to decide whether to follow the consideration she had received on the phone, that is, not to talk to other people about the finding until she was certain of the whole story, or to seek other opinions. For now, since Omiya was only twenty minutes away, she decided that she would devote herself only to her loved ones.

Luna's family home was in an affluent condominium located in the heart of Omiya, an area renowned for its vibrancy and convenient central location, full of stores, restaurants, and close to major transportation lines. The building, an imposing modern structure with a glass and steel facade, reflected the elegance and prestige of the area.

Upon entering the apartment building, Luna walked through a

spacious lobby, elegantly decorated with green plants, designer seating, and contemporary artwork that gave the space a cozy and refined atmosphere. The lobby was always impeccably maintained, with a helpful doorman warmly greeting residents and visitors.

Taking the elevator to the fifth floor, Luna arrived at the apartment where her mother and sister Emi lived.

The apartment opened to a bright entryway, with a large mirror reflecting the natural light that filtered through the living room windows. The living room was spacious and warm, furnished with a mix of modern and vintage furniture that told the family's story through the years.

Comfortable armchairs faced a large window that offered a panoramic view of the city below, while the walls were decorated with family photos and travel memories. The kitchen, adjacent to the living room, was modern and functional, equipped with all necessary appliances and decorated in warm tones that invited time together during meals. The two bedrooms were equally cared for, each reflecting the personality of its occupant, with personal details and a warm and welcoming atmosphere.

As soon as Luna opened the door, she was greeted by a delicious smell that immediately brought her back to happy times spent with her family. Her mother prepared oyakodon, one of her favorite dishes. Oyakodon is a comforting and flavorful Japanese dish that consists of a bowl of rice covered with a tender mixture of chicken and egg, slightly sweet and salty, cooked together with onions in a sauce made from dashi, soy, and mirin. This dish, whose name literally means 'parent and child' because of the combination chicken and egg, had always been a symbol of home for Luna, evoking memories of family dinners and quiet evenings. Entering into the kitchen and seeing the table already set, Luna immediately felt more relaxed, knowing that she would have a pleasant, family-friendly evening, enjoying one of the dishes she loves most.

Over dinner she recounted everything she had discovered. Emi was studying engineering, was familiar with the workings of a battery and the advances Volta had brought to science. She did not know the detail of his private life related to Marianna Paris but did not think it impossible.

Instead, she was extremely interested in understanding how the vessel could have arrived in Japan. Volta was a pioneer in electricity: if that boat was in any way related to him, and given the description made by Kyokutei Bakin of an utterly anomalous vessel with no sails or other visible means of locomotion, one might have thought that it was powered by an electric motor. However, the electric motor had been the result of a succession of discoveries and inventions that had taken shape over the course of the nineteenth century: it had all begun in 1821, when Michael Faraday had demonstrated first principle of converting electrical energy into mechanical energy through electromagnetism, paving the way for a revolutionary field of research. A few years later, in 1831, Faraday had taken a further step forward by electromagnetic induction, a milestone that would set the stage for the modern electric motor.

In 1834, on the other side of Europe, in Russia, Moritz Jacobi had developed the first practical electric motor. This innovative device could lift a weight of about 10 to 15 pounds at a speed of one foot per second, a remarkable achievement for the time. But it was not until 1873 that Zénobe Gramme industry with the invention of the first practical and efficient commercial electric motor capable of sustaining continuous industrial work.

Emi explained to Luna, "If it was really such a vessel, Volta would have anticipated electric motor technology by a hundred years and, more important, energy storage technology to a level that is still unattainable today: the best battery can power a boat for no more than 1,000 miles. From Italy to Japan, by ship, at a time when there were no Panama Canal or Suez Canal, the distance could have been 25,000 miles."

"And how long would it have taken?" asked Luna.

"Let's exaggerate and say it traveled at the same speed as a modern dinghy, so 50 miles per hour. That would be 500 hours, about a month, without ever stopping."

"So even today this trip would be impossible?" "With an electric motor, yes," Emi judged, "unless we do not stop often to recharge or use technologies other than batteries and totally unavailable in Volta's time, i.e., photovoltaic panels or combustible cells."

Luna insisted, "And when were these two technologies invented?"

"As for photovoltaics," Emi explained, "it all started in 1839, thanks to a French physicist named Alexandre-Edmond Becquerel. During some experiments in a laboratory, he discovered the photovoltaic effect by accident." Emi paused, making sure Luna followed her.

"What Becquerel noticed," he continued, "was that certain materials could produce small amounts of electric current when exposed to light. It wasn't much at the time, but it was the first time that anyone observed that light could be converted directly into electricity. This was through photovoltaic effect, where photons from sunlight strike a semiconductor material, usually silicon, releasing electrons and creating an electric current. It was not until the 20th century, however, especially after the energy crisis of the 1970s, that there was an enormous push toward renewable energy and photovoltaics became a key technology. In the 1950s, Bell Laboratories developed the first silicon solar cells with sufficient efficiency to power small devices. In the Seventies, with the rising cost of oil, there was a renewed interest in alternative energy."

"Today, photovoltaic panels are composed of many solar cells, which together can generate enough energy to power homes and industries. Technological advances have greatly improved efficiency and reduced costs, making photovoltaics one of the most promising and affordable sources of renewable energy. In addition, new materials such as perovskite are revolutionizing the field, promising even greater efficiencies and lower production costs."

"And what is the fuel cell?" asked Luna.

"To understand fuel cells properly, we need to take a step back and talk about some fundamental experiments," Emi began. "It all starts with Henry Cavendish, in the late 18th century, who discovered that water is composed of oxygen and hydrogen."

Luna, attentive, nodded to encourage Emi to continue. "Subsequently, Antoine Lavoisier, among other things a friend of Volta, helped define hydrogen as a chemical element," Emi continued. "These discoveries are crucial because they lead us directly to the principle of functioning of the fuel cells, which, in a sense, reverses the process of electrolysis."

Emi paused for a moment to catch his breath, then explained further, "In electrolysis, we use electricity to split water molecules into hydrogen and oxygen. Fuel cells do essentially the opposite: they combine hydrogen and oxygen to produce water and, in this process, generate electricity."

"So, a fuel cell uses hydrogen as fuel and oxygen from the air," Emi added, seeing Luna's growing interest. "When these two gases are introduced into the cell, a chemical reaction takes place that produces water, heat and, most importantly, electricity. It's an incredibly clean way to generate power because the only residual product is water."

As she pondered the information, Luna appeared clearly fascinated. "So would fuel cells have been able to store enough energy for such a long journey?" she asked, curious to better understand the potential of this technology.

"Theoretically, yes," Emi replied, "but we have to consider that the first fuel cell was made only in 1838 by Sir William Grove, an English jurist and physicist. His so-called 'gas battery' was a very rudimentary version of modern fuel cells. Grove used four cells in which hydrogen and oxygen were combined to generate electricity and water. Although it was a great step forward, the efficiency and practicality of this device were limited at the time, and it took at least a hundred years before the technology became truly usable.

Luna smiled, reflecting on how close these giants of science were temporally. "Less than forty years elapsed between Utsuro Bune and the official invention of the fuel cell," she said to herself, thinking of Alessandro Volta, a genius of his time and friend of Lavoisier, discoverer of hydrogen. "And who knows," she added thoughtfully, "perhaps Marianna Paris may have played a role in these discoveries as well..."

GENOA, FRENCH EMPIRE

Sunday, September 9, 1798

After the marriage everything changed. Politically and in the relationship with Alessandro.

From Pavia, Marianna had moved to Genoa both to distance herself from the battlefields of Lombardy and to get closer to the sea, where her future experiments would take place.

In 1794, Lombardy was still part of the Duchy of Milan, under the control of the Habsburgs of Austria. However, political and social tensions had increased as the population's discontent with the Austrian government grew.

Meanwhile, the Ligurian Republic was in a phase of instability, with the risk of becoming involved in the conflicts that were troubling Europe.

The situation had changed dramatically in 1796, when Napoleon's troops had invaded Lombardy and defeated the Austrians at the Battle of Lodi. This had marked beginning of the end of Austrian rule in the region and led to the formation of the Cisalpine Republic, which included Lombardy and part of Liguria.

By 1797, the Ligurian Republic had finally been directly involved in the tumultuous events of the time, when Napoleon Bonaparte had imposed his authority over the region and incorporated it into the Ligurian-Cispadanic Republic, a political entity linked to the French Empire.

It seemed to Marianna that this upheaval in the political situation of the region was only a detail compared to what had taken place in her private life. Only in her mind had she deluded herself that Alessandro's marriage was a mere formality.

Her feelings for Alessandro had not changed, but everything had changed for him, both on the sentimental level and on the scientific collaboration.

The rotor experiment had been the last one they had carried out together, then Marianna had found a space of her own.

She was not sailing in gold, and her workshop also served as her home. It was a modest corner, with windows so dirty that they barely let in the light needed to distinguish objects, and a wooden floor that creaked under his tired footsteps.

The cluttered shelves overflowed with corroded instruments and test tubes that held remnants of past experiments, all covered with a layer of dust that made old objects indistinguishable from new ones.

The air was impregnated with a strong smell of chemicals, with an undertone of burnt wood from an ancient coal stove. Yellowing books and manuscripts were piled in a corner, evidence of the long hours Marianna spent studying and experimenting.

To support herself, Marianna worked as a waitress, and Volta passed on to her a portion of the income derived from the inventions they had developed together. Although the conditions were not the best, that laboratory was the place Marianna really felt at home, where she could experience the potential of extraordinary discoveries every day. It was exactly the kind of space she had always dreamed of: a place of her own where she could experiment and, perhaps, make a difference. Alessandro was ready to tell the world about the invention of the battery while she had continued her studies of the electric motor. She had created smaller and more powerful ones, optimizing the positioning of the magnets and the path that the copper wires followed outside the rotor, but the limit was always the same: the batteries ran out almost immediately. She was ready to try the electric motor linked to a propeller in a boat but the risk of being without propulsion in the open sea was too high.

She had to find way to store and harness energy more efficiently. Alessandro had given him the idea during one of their now rare conversations. During an experiment, Alessandro had tried dipping the electrodes (i.e., anode and cathode, connected to the negative and positive poles of the battery, respectively) into a glass of water. Nothing had happened. He had then brought the anode and cathode close together until they were almost touching, and the passage of current had begun. His curiosity had then led him to perform the same experiment using salt water, and everything had changed. The current flow had started immediately, even with the electrodes far apart, but the most interesting thing had been noticing that bubbles were forming on anode and cathode.

Alessandro was an avid scholar of any new discoveries, and his contacts throughout Europe enabled him to keep abreast of the latest developments in chemical studies.

He had especially had a close correspondence with Antoine Lavoisier, until the French Revolution had written one of its darkest pages, leading him to the guillotine and causing irreparable loss to the scientific community.

Lavoisier had told him about the studies of Carl Wilhelm Scheele and Henry Cavendish who, about two decades earlier, had discovered two gases called oxygen and hydrogen.

In 1766 Cavendish was conducting experiments on acidification, including hydrochloric acid (then known as 'muriatic acid'), in combination with various metals.

During his experiments, Cavendish noticed the formation of a gas that burned with a clear flame and, in the presence of oxygen, produced water vapor. This gas had not been previously identified and, therefore, Cavendish called it 'flammable air.'

Cavendish continued to investigate the properties of this gas and discovered that it reacted with oxygen to form water when passed through a flame.

Later, Lavoisier demonstrated that Cavendish's flammable air consisted mainly of hydrogen. It was Lavoisier who coined the term 'hydrogen,' which was derived from ancient Greek and meant 'water maker,' since hydrogen is involved in the formation of water during combu- stion.

In his famous 1789 treatise 'Traité Élémentaire de Chimie,' Lavoisier presented water as a compound of hydrogen and oxygen and provided a detailed explanation of the chemical reactions involved.

Alessandro had been fascinated by this text and by the further explanations that his friend Lavoisier had communicated to him by letter. Ah, how many further magnificent discoveries it would have brought to science if the French had not gone mad!

The moment Alessandro saw bubbles near the two electrodes in water, he therefore knew perfectly well that the water was composed of hydrogen and oxygen, and that the hydrogen was flammable.

The next step, which was to identify as hydrogen the gas at the cathode (the negative pole of the battery) and oxygen at the anode (the positive pole), was not a complicated step for his brilliant mind. It would take many more years for the chemical reaction to be formalized in detail involved but Alessandro now had a way to isolate hydrogen and oxygen.

As Alessandro recounted these wonders, Marianna's eyes sparkled with joy at receiving all that knowledge, and her brain was already at work: if it takes the electrical energy stored in the battery to split water into hydrogen and oxygen, joining hydrogen and oxygen would eventually create electrical energy as well as water.

She had not done university studies but the process was logical to her mentally, she now had to try to actually use it.

She did not share this idea with Alessandro, at least not right away.

In her laboratory she set to work. The first result was to repeat Alessandro's experiment and succeed in collecting a good amount of hydrogen and oxygen. The next step was to insert a membrane between the anode, to which she connected the oxygen source, and the cathode, to which she connected the hydrogen source.

When hydrogen reached the anode by crossing the membrane, water droplets formed at the cathode, and the electroscope signaled the passage of electric current.

The miracle had occurred.

OMIYA, JAPAN

Thursday, January 17, 2019

During dinner, the topic of Utsuro Bune was set aside. Luna, despite frequent visits home, made an effort not to monopolize the conversation with her interests. As she continued chatting, she noticed that her oyakodon was getting cold.

Savoring another bite of the oyakodon, Luna could not help but express her admiration, "Mom, every time you prepare it, it tastes even better. I don't know how you manage to do everything the same as before, despite the wheelchair."

Mother answered her with a sweet smile, "Well, everything is not quite the same as before. We lowered the stove and arranged things in the lower shelves to make it easier for me, but I still need help from Emi-chan from time to time."

"I'm sorry I can't come more often to help you," Luna said with an edge of sadness in her voice.

Emi promptly intervened, "Luna-chan, don't even think about it. Everything is fine here at home. You have work and university to manage. And the financial contribution you send is more than enough for us."

"I know but I wish I could do more," replied Luna.

Her mother looked at her with a somewhat sad look, "I'm sorry I became a burden to you. I hope I wasn't the cause of the end of your relationship with Gabriele. I'm really happy that you two have started talking to each other again."

Luna stared at her mother with wistful eyes. It pained her to give her mom the impression that she was a burden. It had now been almost two years since that car accident in which her father had lost his life and her mother had been paralyzed from the waist down but, every time she saw the sadness in her mom's eyes, she felt like going back to that phone call in which Emi told her to rush to the hospital.

She told her, "Mom, I have told you many times already. You are not the cause of anything, really, stop thinking otherwise. Things between Gabriele and me went as they were supposed to go. And no, we haven't started talking regularly again; I just asked him for help with my research."

The mother smiled fondly at her, albeit with a hint of skepticism, "It doesn't seem to me that there was any need to contact him specifically just because an Italian flag was found. With the Internet, you could have handled your research directly from Japan. However, as I have already told you, I am glad that there was at least this contact. I never understood why you decided to sever all relations so abruptly."

"Our separation was painful," Luna explained, trying to keep calm. "It was a consensual but still a difficult decision. And now is no chance of things going back to the way they were. In fact, even this afternoon we ended up arguing on the phone."

"What do you mean?" intervened Emi, clearly concerned about her sister.

"He started being a smartass as usual, one of the things that always annoyed me about him," Luna said with an edge of irritation in her voice. "Finally, I hung on him."

"Oh, you poor thing!" exclaimed Mom, visibly upset by the situation.

"Forget it," Luna cut short, changing her tone. "He'll get over it. Can we change the subject now?"

After a brief moment of silence, Mom decided to turn the conversation toward a lighter topic. "How's work going?" she asked, trying to sound as natural as possible.

Luna smiled, regaining some enthusiasm. "Lately I was getting a little bored in the library but then I had an idea that rekindled my interest. I talked to Kato-san about the possibility of researching the Satake clan, thinking of using what I find out as a topic for one of our monthly lectures," she explained. "As soon as I mentioned this idea, Kato-san showed incredible interest and encouraged me to start right away."

With a flicker of pride in her eyes, she continued, "He also gave me a few days off to devote to research and talked to the director of the Choshi Library, who offered to help me. It is inspiring to see so much enthusiasm around the project, and with the discoveries I have already made, I am convinced that the conference will be a great success."

Emi, impressed by Luna's passion, wasted no time and jokingly asked, "So, is there a promotion on the horizon?"

Luna laughed slightly, shaking her head. "No, I'm not interested in a promotion. You know that this is only temporary employment for me. Once I graduate, my goal is to become a teacher. That's my real dream."

Emi nodded, fascinated by her sister's enthusiasm. "Understand, it's good to see how dedicated you are to this project. Who knows, maybe this research will open new doors for you in the future."

Luna smiled again, feeling Emi's support. "Yes, I hope so. Meanwhile, I want to do my best with this conference and find out all I can about the Satake clan and the Utsuro Bune. It's a unique opportunity and I want to make the most of it."

TOKYO, JAPAN

Friday, May 6, 2016

Golden Week is one of the most anticipated holiday periods in Japan, a week in which several national holidays follow one another, allowing many Japanese to enjoy a break from work and daily commitments. This week is marked by a significant increase in domestic and international tourism, with many people taking the opportunity to travel, relax, and participate in events and celebrations.

In 2016, Golden Week began on April 29 and ended on May 5, including four major holidays.

The week began with Shōwa Day, celebrated on April 29, a day dedicated to Emperor Shōwa's (Hirohito's) birthday, a time to reflect on his long regency and the events that marked Japan during his reign.

May 3 had been Constitution Memorial Day, commemorating the enactment of the Japanese Constitution in 1947.

The following day, May 4, was Green Day, a holiday dedicated to nature and the environment. This day encouraged many people to go outdoor, visit parks and gardens, and participate in ecological activities, emphasizing the importance of environmental awareness.

The week ended on May 5 with Children's Day, known as Kodomo no Hi. This day was dedicated to children, particularly boys, and was celebrated with displays of carp-shaped flags (koinobori), which symbolized strength and success in growing up.

On Friday, May 6, 2016, the Golden Week festivities were over but that day proved to be one of the most important in Gabriele's life.

On April 22, Gabriele had returned to Italy for one of the many work commitments that required his presence. Toyota was finally being convinced to adopt a new technology that Gabriele had been promoting for several months. However, before making a final decision, the Japanese executives wanted to visit the headquarters laboratories to personally verify the validity of the results so extolled by Gabriele. As a typical salesman, Gabriele tended to emphasize the merits and underestimate the risks of the new technology, but he knew that, with Japanese customers, he could not exaggerate; sooner or later they would notice and no longer trust him.

During his first week in Italy, Gabriele had spent all his time with clients between meetings, dinners, and visits to suppliers. He did not mind that routine; in fact, he found it very constructive. These occasions allowed him to approach clients in a way that would have been impossible in formal situations. In particular, dinners had the same value as a meeting or a positive test report. His clients also knew this and played along, especially when it came to pretending to slightly lose control after a grappa or limoncello, creating an atmosphere of trust and intimacy, albeit temporarily.

The second week, coinciding with Golden Week, he was free instead and had decided to spend as much time possible with his family. His mom had greeted him with a plate of spaghetti with bolognese sauce, far the food he missed most in Japan. It wasn't that he couldn't find bolognese sauce in restaurants, or that he couldn't cook it himself, but his mom's was special. What was the ingredient secret, he would not find out even after many years. It could have been the sausage he put in the pot in chunks, or the hours spent in the pressure cooker, or perhaps the fact that there were no onions or carrots, thus enhancing the taste of the meat and tomato sauce.

He suspected that the secret ingredient, however, was in the fact that it was his own mother who had cooked it for him.

Unfortunately, he could not stay in Italy for the last weekend: the end of Golden Week coincided with the return so many Japanese from vacation, causing flight prices to soar. Tickets cost twice as much as normal, exceeding his budget. Thus, on the afternoon of May 5, Gabriele hugged his mother and sister and took off from Milan for Japan.

The flight went well as usual. He had a premium economy ticket that, although it did not offer business class meals (which he did not care for), gave him the legroom he needed and access to the lounge, which was very convenient for relaxing before the flight. After a three-hour layover in Paris, he departed again for Tokyo. Twelve hours later, he landed at Haneda Airport.

Gabriele had seen many airports but Haneda was by far his favorite. In addition to Japanese perfection in management, Haneda offered the convenience of being directly connected to the Tokyo subway. In only thirty minutes he could be home, avoiding long transfers that often characterized other international airports. This was a huge advantage, especially after a long intercontinental flight.

He quickly passed through the controls and at 11:30 a.m. got off the Yamanote line at Ebisu Station, where he was greeted by the reassuring jingle of that station.

Tokyo's train stations were known for their distinctive jingles, short tunes that signaled the arrival and departure of trains. These jingles were not only useful for informing passengers but became an integral part of the local culture, each with a unique melody that often reflected the character of the neighborhood in which the station was located. The jingles also served to lend a touch of humanity and warmth to an otherwise very mechanical and impersonal transportation system.

The Ebisu station jingle was especially loved by residents and travelers. The tune was taken from an old advertisement for beer produced by Yebisu Beer, a historic Japanese brewery that had given its name to the quarter. Whenever Gabriele heard that jingle, he was reminded of the cozy atmosphere of Ebisu's pubs and restaurants, a place that combined Tokyo's modernity with a touch of tradition. It was a sound he now associated with returning home, with tranquility after a long day.

Another very famous jingle was from the Takadanobaba station, whose story Luna had told him about: This station used a tune from the anime 'Astro Boy' (Tetsuwan Atom), an homage to Osamu Tezuka's famous manga. The choice was particularly significant, considering that Tezuka had set many of his stories in this very neighborhood.

Just outside the station, he considered getting a meal at the McDonald's across the street, knowing that he would find nothing to eat at home. However, he decided to get to the apartment first and then decide what to do. Thus, he proceeded, dragging his heavy trolley.

He crossed a couple of streets and saw the Tako Koen, the octopus park, so called because of the octopus-shaped game whose tentacles created slides on which children had fun. He was about to take the last street before arriving home when he heard calling his name. "Gabriele-chan!"

He turned around, trying to figure out where that voice was coming from. "I'm here!"

He oriented himself better, focused and saw her swinging on the swing of the small park.

"Luna? What are you doing here?" asked, his mood quickly shifting from surprise to concern, then turning to happiness when he recognized her reassuring smile.

Luna stopped rocking and ran to him. "I missed you," she said, hugging him.

"But how long have you been here? You could have called me and told me..." Luna blocked him. "Shut up," and kissed him.

GENOA, FRENCH EMPIRE

Thursday, January 9, 1800

It's unbelievable!" said Alessandro, his hands resting on the machine, his eyes wide with amazement. "But how did you do it!"

The blade was rotating at high speed, smoothly. They had not worked together with the electric motor a couple of years before but this one was not connected to any battery!

"I am a scientist, I have never considered this possibility but I have to ask you this question: are you a witch? Does it work with magic?" He joked, but up to a point.

Their meetings had become more and more infrequent; Alessandro had recently presented to the world their pile, which was obviously named Volta's pile. Alessandro was on top of the world: invited by kings and emperors, governments all over Europe vied for his presence and explanation of his inventions, his fame would last forever. Marianna was jealous. Of course, not because of the name they had given to their pile. She was a woman; even she did not consider having that kind of recognition. All she needed was the personal satisfaction in continuing her inventions, and perhaps bring some progress to civilization, even if nobody had never known her name.

She was jealous of Alessandro. From his wife to the governments, everyone demanded him and he had less and less time for her. There was still affection between them but it was now only platonic and scientific.

She had invited him that evening because she had to show him her creation. Over the past two years the progress had been incredible: a year earlier he had made hydrogen react with oxygen and activated an electroscope. Then she had switched to the electric motor, with much longer lifetimes than she could achieve with batteries. But that had not been enough for her: creating hydrogen was very expensive and dangerous to process. During one test, a container caught fire and had burned two fingers.

After several trials, she had managed to achieve the same result by using, instead of hydrogen, a much less dangerous and more readily available substance: methanol.

She had been unable to understand the reason for the result; she had to assume that there was some component in ethanol that, reacting to oxygen, generated electricity as hydrogen did but in a much more efficient way.

Marianna patiently explained the whole process to Alessandro.

As he listened, Alessandro's expression changed from astonishment, to wonder, to thoughtfulness, and finally to worry.

"Marianna, you are a genius," he finally said, "but be very careful! You have no idea what's going on politically behind the pile, an invention that is certainly innovative but much more backward than this... How did you call it?"

"Methanol cell," Marianna replied.

"...this Methanol Cell. The French government already has me contacted by an artillery general to find possible practical applications. For now, it seems that the general André Masséna will use the pile to power light signal towers on the border with Austria, but it won't be long before they invent lethal uses. Imagine if they got their hands on this... What to call it? An almost infinite source of energy?"

Marianna shielded herself, "Exaggerated, it's not infinite! But I would have some ideas..."

"It doesn't matter if it's infinite or not. Look at the French, how they use science: they cut off Lavoisier's head, the greatest scientist in their history, and as soon as they got their hands on the pile, they found a military application for it."

"And what am I supposed to do? Stop experimenting?" asked Marianna rhetorically.

"Be careful, don't tell anyone what you are doing. When the time will be right, I'll help you to decide how to proceed, and this time it will to be all in your name, you'll end up in the history books." He smiled at her.

Marianna hugged him tightly, now the height of their physical contact. In her head, however, she was already thinking about how Alessandro would react when she managed to develop what she had planned, an almost infinite source of energy...

MILAN, ITALY

Monday, January 21, 2019

Gabriele had been nervous all weekend. He had not heard from Luna and felt resentful toward her. He had lost hours of work and sleep to help her in her search, and she had hung up on him. What had he done to offend her? All right, the explanation about Occam's Razor could have been spared. He knew that being know-it-all was a flaw of his; he paid attention to it and tried to avoid it as much as possible but, every once in a while, he couldn't refrain. After all, it was only a small flaw and Luna might as well have glossed over it.

As he thought back to the incident, he wondered if he had run out. Perhaps he had been too direct, or perhaps Luna was facing a difficult moment and he had not realized it. Still, he could not help but feel frustrated. He had really tried to help her, and his reaction seemed unjustified to him.

So there had to be more to it. His remark casts doubt on the possibility that the woman in the Utsuro Bune was really Marianna Paris. But what was so important? Luna had still made an exceptional discovery, and the fact that she did not know for sure the woman's nationality did not detract from her work at all!

For three days, Gabriele had been repeating this himself over and over again, trying to calm himself after his last phone call with Luna. However, every time he tried to convince himself, an inner little voice reminded him of two obvious facts: first, knowing for sure the woman's nationality would have a huge impact on public reaction to the presentation of the discovery, especially whether the woman came from a distant part of the world; second, he also wanted to find out the truth.

His mind kept returning to those thoughts, making him ponder how important this information really was. He knew that certainty would add value to Luna's discovery but there was also his personal desire to know. Perhaps his approach had been too direct and saccharine but his interest was genuine.

Gabriele realized that he could not ignore her emotional involvement. He really wanted to help Luna unravel the mystery of the Utsuro Bune and perhaps he should have found a better way to communicate with her while avoiding hurting her feelings.

He decided that there were two methods to unravel the situation: an empathic one, in which he would call Luna and express his feelings; and a rational one, in which he would bring Luna new information to help her in her search. Undoubtedly, he discarded the empathic solution and started thinking about how he could search for new information. Although the empathic approach might have helped to resolve misunderstandings between them, his practical and analytical nature led him to choose concrete action.

On Sunday morning he set to work, alternating between times when he strolled back and forth around the living room and times when he raked the miniature Zen Garden. He decided to start from the assumption that Luna was right.

Marianna had arrived in Japan in February 1803. The last historical information about her was from 1792 and was taken from an exchange of letters with Alessandro Volta. This meant that Marianna must have left for Japan between 1792 and the end of 1802. Indeed, she had brought with her a flag that did not exist before 1797, so the departure could not have been earlier than that year. At that moment, it was not important to understand how or why he had undertaken that journey but only to accept that it had happened. One thing was certain: such a feat could not have gone unnoticed at the time; therefore, there had to be other sources documenting it.

Gabriele decided to focus on the region between Pavia, where Marianna had met Volta, and Genoa, a probable point of departure by ship to the ocean. Therefore, he pointed to France, which controlled that region at the time, as a possible source of information.

His role in the company entailed responsibilities that sometimes did not allow him to sleep at night but also freedom, which he took advantage of when necessary. He knew that he would have no unavoidable commitments at the office that Monday, so after sending a brief email to his boss from the phone, he took the train to Milan, bound for the French consulate. He had visited the consulate's website the previous evening, without finding any reference to cultural sections, or the like, that could direct him in his search. He hoped to find an archive, a library, or some useful resource. He had then written to a generic email address asking if he could be received the next day to discuss a research paper he was working on. He did not hold out much hope of being received, but he thought that by showing up in person, he might arouse a modicum of compassion and get information that by email would never come.

By a fluke of fate, he knew exactly where the French consulate was located: right across the street from the Japanese consulate, where he had been several times to obtain the necessary visa for his stay in Japan.

Arriving at Milan's Central Station, Gabriele started to walk to the French consulate. Twenty-five minutes of walking took him through the park of Republic Square, where he decided to stop for a break, deciding whether to opt for a second breakfast or a Genoese focaccia. It was 10 a.m., so he opted for a second breakfast of cappuccino and brioche.

He had informed the consulate that he would show up around 11 a.m., so he had plenty of time to relax. He stopped at a cafe with outdoor tables and enjoyed the cool winter sun on his face. The park in Republic Square was bare, the little snow that had fallen in the previous days had completely melted but sitting outside and enjoying a warm cappuccino was one of the pleasures of winter.

As he sipped his cappuccino, Gabriele imagined what he would have said to the consulate if he had found an interlocutor willing to listen. "I think that, in the early 1800s, Alessandro Volta's mistress took a vessel and went to Japan. Do you have anywhere records in which I can find evidence of this trip?" He knew that this approach risked having him viewed at best as a waste of time, at worst as a fool.

He thought of a vaguer version, "I am collaborating with a Japanese library on some research related to the period of the Cisalpine Republic, particularly relating to trade and shipping. Are there any archives you can suggest for me to collect documents?" Yes, sounded better.

With the cappuccino now finished and the brioche enjoyed, he felt invigorated and ready to continue. He paid his bill and resumed the walk to the consulate, feeling the energy of the coffee warm his soul and determination grow with each step. Arriving at the majestic building of the French consulate, he paused for a moment to gather his thoughts and breathe deeply. He walked in and approached the information desk, explaining the reason for his visit. The receptionist listened to him to the end and then asked only, "Do you have an appointee?"

"Not really, I wrote an email but…"

"I'm sorry, without an appointment you can't…"

"Are you Gabriele?" The receptionist was interrupted by a voice behind Gabriele's back, with a strong French accent.

"Yes, that's me," replied Gabriele, confused.

"Nice to meet you, I'm Marie Durand, the consulate press secretary," Marie said as she extended her hand.

"Nice to meet you" Gabriele replied, squeezing her. He observed her and noticed that she must have been in her mid-thirties, and she had a warm and welcoming smile. She had long brown hair pulled back into a ponytail, which highlighted her delicate face and brown eyes bright with intelligence and curiosity.

"When I got to the office this morning, I saw your email and it intrigued me," she told him. "Most of all, I was struck by the optimism in writing to a public agency on sunday night and hoping to have an appointment on Monday morning." She smiled.

Gabriele returned the smile. "Did you see that it worked?"

Marie added, "Unfortunately, though, I can't devote time to her today and have her sit in the office, but perhaps I can help you anyway. Can you tell me more about what you are looking for?" Gabriele felt a little uncomfortable discussing standing in the consulate lobby with people coming and going. However, he understood that he was already lucky to have someone to talk to. "A friend in Japan works in a library, and every month they cover historical topics little known to their audience. The spring agenda includes a theme on the Cisalpine Republic, so she asked me for help in finding some documents, particularly related to sea travel and trade."

"Yes, for these generic topics, what I had in mind really fits the bill," Marie said. "A few years ago, a group of students put online all the historical documents that were in danger of being lost because of their, shall we say, little relevance. They are good sources to get an idea of the day-to-day situation in the past. The only problem is that they started with documents dated as of Jan. 1, 1800." Gabriele thought about this for a moment: the Utsuro Bune event had occurred in early 1803; even though Phileas Fogg and Passepartout's trip around the world was still seventy years away, he speculated that Marianna's trip could not have lasted more than two years, so it could not have been before 1800.

"This should not be a problem," said Gabriele. "But do they affect the whole French empire?"

"I think," Marie replied. "At least the European continental one."

"That would be great..."

Marie added, "On the site you must register and apply for login credentials, but since you have come this far, I am leaving you with temporary credentials that are valid for one week. If you then want to continue accessing the site, you will have to apply to the organization that runs it."

Marie gave him a note with website address and credentials, her business card, best wishes for successful research, and a request, "Let me know how the research is going and also information about the event the library will organize in Japan. I might write a nice post about it!"

Gabriele thanked her so much and confirmed that she would

be kept up to date, although a little embarrassed because he already knew he could not do it, since the event in Japan was his invention.

He exited the building and, seeing the Japanese consulate in front of him, he got a craving for ramen. Fortunately, Milan was spoiled for choice, so after a quick search on his cell phone, he walked to a small eatery that had his favorite tonkotsu ramen, on the menu.

Gabriele sat down at the table in the small restaurant and, while watching the cook behind the counter, a steaming bowl of tonkotsu ramen was placed in front of him.

The broth was thick and opalescent, a symphony of flavors obtained from hours of slow cooking of the pork bones, which had released all their rich collagen and flavor. Gabriele observed the tiny fat bubbles dancing on the surface, promising a velvety, enveloping texture. The noodles, slightly al dente, were submerged in that precious liquid, ready to absorb every drop of flavor.

Above the broth, a meticulous arrangement of toppings caught the eye: tender, lightly caramelized slices of roasted pork rested next to a seared egg, the yolk creamy and barely gelatinous. Thin slices of fresh spring onion added a note of freshness, while shiitake mushrooms and bamboo shoots brought an earthy, delicate complexity.

Gabriele lifted the sticks, grabbing a pile of noodles and dipping them once more into the broth before bringing them to his mouth. The flavor was explosive, a perfect combination of umami, sweetness and a hint of savoriness. The warmth of the broth warmed his tired body, and with each mouthful he felt more and more invigorated.

When he walked out of the restaurant into chilly January air, ramen still warmed him from the inside.

Ninety minutes later he was home again, sitting at his desk. He had taken a day off work but, nonetheless, he felt compelled to check his cell phone and pc. Not that anyone was imposing it on him, but leaving too many emails unanswered would have made the next day untenable. Moreover, the very little autonomy of some of his co-workers risked slowing down important activities.

He scrolled through the emails, responding only to those that required short answers, neglecting the longer and more complex ones that could wait until the next day. A couple of hours later, he finally turned off his work PC and turned on his personal one, ready to devote himself to the most interesting topic.

He typed in the site address, entered the credentials, and was faced with the first obstacle, obvious but not considered: it was all in French. He passed a couple of menus with the help of Google Translator and arrived at a very intuitive search engine. He had to enter the time frame of the desired document, the source, and the text to be searched.

He selected the period between Jan. 1, 1800, and Feb. 22, 1803 (the date the Utsuro Bune landed in Japan) and did not indicate any specific sources so as not to exclude potentially interesting documents. As for what text to look for, the issue was more complicated.

Started with 'Japon' but got zero results. He realized, however, that he did not know exactly what kind of documents to expect; therefore, he decided to leave the text field blank and started the search.

After a few moments, the screen became populated with results. Gabriele began scrolling through the headlines, many of which concerned trade, diplomatic reports, and chronicles of local events. One in particular caught his attention for its simplicity and normality: 'Rapport de Vol' dated 1802. He opened it, curious to see how an ordinary theft was documented at the time.

The document, written in formal French, reported the report of a citizen, one Monsieur Pierre Dubois, who complained that his pocket watch had been stolen while walking through a crowded square. The description was dictated and precise: Dubois explained that the watch was a family gift, with a special engraving on the back. He described the suspect as a man of medium height, with dark hair and smart clothes, who had disappeared into the crowd after bumping into him seemingly by accident.

The report continued with statements from witnesses, some of whom had noticed the suspicious man prowling the area for some time. One witness in particular, a flower vendor, had seen the man walking away in a hurry immediately after the incident. The local police had promised to investigate but the document reported no further developments. Gabriele found it interesting to read such an everyday document. The description of the theft, the reaction of the person involved, and the formal language used in the report gave him a glimpse of life in the past. It was not what he was looking for but he still appreciated the opportunity to immerse himself in a real and tangible piece of history.

He tried several combinations of text again.

'Marianna' + 'Paris': 25 results, all related to the Marianne of France and Paris.

'Boat': 431 results. Too many. He tried again with 'ship', 'vessel' and all the synonyms Google could suggest to him. Too many results.

What was special about the description he had read of the Utsuro Bune?

Google came to his rescue again:

the word "sphere" can be translated into French in different ways depending on the context. Here are some common translations:

Sphère - Used primarily to denote a geometrical sphere or spherical object.

Globe - Used to refer to a terrestrial or celestial globe.

Boule - Indicates a ball or sphere in a more informal context, like a game ball.

Domaine - Can be used metaphorically to indicate a field or sphere of activity (e.g., "domaine d'expertise").

Univers - Figuratively, it can be used to indicate a sphere of influence or a domain (e.g., "univers des idées").

He typed 'Sphére' + 'Bateau'. Zero results. Of course: wrong accent.

He typed 'Sphère+ 'Bateau'.

One single result.

Heartbeat accelerated, trembling index finger he clicked the link, copied the text of the page and pasted it into Google Translator:

'Minutes of the Maritime Police of Genoa, Cisalpine Republic.

Date: 12 June 1802

Subject: Report of an unknown spherical object in the waters of Genoa

At 8:00 a.m. on June 11, 1802, some local fishermen filed a complaint regarding the sighting of an unknown sphere-shaped monster speeding fast and silently near their vessels. The witnesses, experienced and well-known fishermen in the community, reported observing the unknown being moving with unnatural speed, producing no noise.

Mr. Marco Boni, one of the fishermen, described the object as a large sphere three-quarters submerged, visible only as a shadow in the dark of night. Another, Pietro Ferraro, has confirmed the sighting, adding that the object appeared to follow a precise trajectory, deftly avoiding ships.

We would not have given credence to these reports except that this is the third such report that has been received in the past month. Previously, on May 5 and May 24, 1802, other fishermen reported sightings of a similar spherical object in the same waters.

Given the unusual and recurring nature of these reports, further investigation is deemed necessary. It is suggested that the object could be a new secret weapon or an unknown craft. Therefore, we recommend sending a team to verify and, if possible, retrieve the object for further examination.

Signed,

Capitaine François Dupont Maritime Police of Genoa'

Gabriele looked at the motionless screen: a spherical-shaped vessel was roaming the waters off Genoa eight months before a spherical-shaped vessel with a Western occupant landed in Japan.

It might not have been definitive confirmation that Marianna Paris was on that boat, but he was practically certain now that that boat had departed from Genoa, with a red-haired woman as its only guest, with an Italian flag inside, with Marianna Paris's name written on it.

He thought about the next steps: he would not inform Luna yet; he wanted to try to give her more information. If he could not find it, he would only send her this report.

He thought about what was missing to close the circle and gave himself two answers: he had the who and the when; he lacked the how and the why. He left the how in the background for a moment and focused on the why: why would someone, in the early 19th century, leave Genoa and go to Japan with a strange craft?

He paced back and forth across the room but space was beginning to run out for him. It was 6:30 in the afternoon, it was completely dark outside and evidently cold but he put on a jacket and went out into the garden.

The sprinkling of snow had completely disappeared, leaving the garden in a winter stillness. The raspberry plants, pruned in the fall, were resting, ready to become themselves lushly in the spring. The cherry tree was alone and bare, its branches bare against the winter sky. It approached the little tree, not very tall, perhaps reaching five feet. Its branches, wide and open like an umbrella, seemed to welcome the cold with patience.

He touched it gently, imagining the feeling he would have when, in a couple of months, he would begin to see the first buds. He visualized the day when, raising the shutters, he would see the flowers bloom in all their beauty. The thought filled him with sweet anticipation, knowing that that moment would mark the beginning of a new season, full of color and life.

TOKYO, JAPAN

Saturday, April 1, 2017

"Roppongi? But there are no parks here," said Gabriele. "Oof!" Luna huffed. "Do you trust me or not? Follow me and you'll see." Gabriele smiled and followed her.

The cherry trees had blossomed only the previous Thursday, and that weekend all the parks in Tokyo would be crowded with people fighting for a place under the most beautiful trees to picnic and enjoy the most distinctive event of the year.

They, like the previous year, would also participate in the picnic at Yoyogi Park together with their friends. After drawing lots, Marta and Davide had won the honor of waking up at dawn to search for the best possible cherry tree for their picnic. By 7:30 a.m. they had sent a photo to confirm that the mission had been successfully accomplished.

Upon learning that they had avoided that responsibility, and would therefore have the morning off, Luna had asked Gabriele to follow her to a 'secret place' where she said the best view of cherry trees in all of Tokyo could be seen.

That was an important statement.

If it had been true, such a place would have been in all guidebooks, but Gabriele had never heard of it.

Until then, the places that Gabriele would have felt like recommending to see the best cherry blossoms were two: the steep meadow next to the imperial palace, where small rowboats sailed under a shower of petals, and the so-called Blue Cave, an area on the Meguro River where the fronds of the trees touched above the river, as if to create a suspended cave, and at night were illuminated with blue light, creating the magical atmosphere that gave the event its name.

Both offered incredible views, which alone were worth a trip to Japan. However, they had the only flaw of being famous and mentioned in many guidebooks, making them rather crowded and difficult to fully enjoy.

If the place mentioned by Luna had really existed and really been better than the Imperial Meadow and the Blue Cave, it would have been a true hidden gem, a secret corner that only a lucky few could discover and appreciate in its full beauty.

His bewilderment had increased when they had gotten off the Nanboku Line at Roppongi-Itchome station. That was a neighborhood of offices, embassies, and residences of the highest order. For these reasons, he had never gotten off at that station, preferring the nearby Roppongi station, which was much more practical for frequenting the nightlife area.

The station was modern, like the entire Nanboku Line, one of the last subway lines built in the metropolis. Its recent construction was immediately noticeable thanks to automatic doors on the tracks, which ensured the of waiting passengers, and the spacious and well-maintained spaces. After a couple of levels of escalators (being the last line built, the Nanboku Line was dug very deep), they arrived at the station concourse. Here, they could admire an artificial waterfall cascading down from a stone wall, lending a touch of nature amid the modern architecture. They passed through a small shopping mall with upscale stores and various Western-style dishes.

It was evident that this was a neighborhood of embassies and residences of foreigners.

Gabriele took mental note of the variety of stores and restaurants. That place could have been useful for shopping and trying something different.

Having crossed the small but elegant shopping area, they took two more flights of escalators and found themselves on a modern pedestrian walkway of steel and glass that crossed two small streets and led directly to a complex of buildings visible just outside the station.

Just as Gabriele turned to Luna, ready to throw another dig her about the impossibility of finding there the place she described, he stopped short and realized why she had brought him there.

The road under the footbridge was a small avenue lined with broad-leafed cherry trees, which closed to form a kind of flowering gallery. He had perhaps seen such lush ones before, but the special aspect was that, being on the walkway, they were just below the branches, even being able to reach out and touch them with his hands. They were immersed in the flowers, completely surrounded, being able to admire a quantity of petals like never. The bloom was already a special event, but he never thought he would feel so enveloped as he was at that moment.

"Well? Don't you talk anymore?" taunted Luna.

"Thank you, I had never seen anything like and never thought I would." That was all Gabriele felt like saying. They stayed a few minutes cuddled together enjoying the view, then walked to the complex of buildings at the end of the walkway to enjoy croissants and hood overlooking the avenue.

At 11 a.m. they returned to the station via the footbridge again. Gabriele stopped and said to her, "Don't tell anyone else about this place, otherwise in a few years we won't even be able to get on the footbridge anymore."

Luna smiled. "Okay, it's our secret, and of the thousands of people who pass through here every day on their way to work."

GENOA, FRENCH REPUBLIC

Thursday, November 4, 1802

Alessandro paced back and forth nervously in the room, his footsteps echoing on the wooden floor. Marianna had never seen him so agitated but understood perfectly well the reasons for it. The tension in the air was palpable, so much so that it seemed to stifle any attempt at conversation.

They had discovered it. Perhaps some spy had noticed the strange craft moving very fast at sea, and the government had begun to investigate. She was always looking for hidden places to carry out her tests but, evidently, she had not been careful enough.

Fortunately, Alessandro had his own contacts. Over the years, he had managed to weave a network of acquaintances among French politicians, scientists, and officers. One evening, during a diplomatic dinner, he had picked up a conversation between two maritime police officers. They were talking about a mysterious object sighted near the coast of Genoa and a red-haired woman who seemed to be connected to this discovery. Alessandro had immediately realized that it was Marianna.

Alessandro had befriended a middle-ranking official, Charles Moreau, during an official visit to Paris. Moreau, a man of gentle manners but sharp wit, was always seeking personal favors and advantages. Alessandro decided to take advantage of this weakness. One evening, he invited Moreau to dinner at an elegant restaurant in Genoa. Between glasses of wine, Alessandro casually mentioned an old friend with whom he was working on a scientific project. He described her as a woman with hair red, intelligent and passionate, hoping Moreau would connect the dots.

Moreau, who was not inclined to keep the information to himself, ended up confessing that there were rumors about a red-haired woman who was attracting the government's attention because of a mysterious boat. The description coincided too much with Marianna's appearance to be a coincidence. Alessandro feigned surprise and concern but inside he knew he had to act quickly.

After dinner, Alessandro met Marianna in her laboratory. He told her everything he had discovered. "Marianna, you are in danger. Someone has noticed your boarding and is investigating you. A spy may have followed you and now you may be under surveillance."

The last two years had been incredible. After methanol she had tried ethanol and realized that, for the same volume, ethanol lasted thirty percent longer.

She had tried other types of alcohol and found that the absolute best was pentanol, with a longer shelf life of an additional ten percent.

She had no practical goals. She just wanted to challenge herself and get farther and farther. Which meant, at this point, wanting to cross the Atlantic.

In the spring of 1801, Marianna had begun experimenting with methanol on a small boat. The tests were dangerous: she could not risk being seen with a boat without oars or sails speeding through the Tyrrhenian Sea. She had to conduct her tests at dawn, before the sea became busy. Despite the risks, Marianna had conducted several tests between Genoa and Corsica, verifying that with methanol she could travel about 1.5 nautical miles per liter.

The liter, the new unit of measurement for liquids just adopted in France, was much more convenient than the old imperial gallon, and Marianna had immediately made it her own. She knew that for a trip from Genoa to Gibraltar, about 1,200 nautical miles, and then from Gibraltar to the United States, another 3,800 nautical miles, she would have to travel a total of 5,000 nautical miles. This meant that it would have needed about 8,000 liters of methanol to get there and back, far too much in terms of production, space, and weight.

Even considering the use of pentanol, which had a slightly higher energy content, none of his calculations led to a consumption of less than 5,000 liters of fuel. The situation remained unsustainable for a transatlantic voyage. Marianna realized that, despite her advances in combustible cell technology, the practical limitations of methanol and pentanol production and storage were a significant obstacle to realizing her dream of efficient long-haul sailing.

She had studied the three alcohols he had tested to figure out how to find a fourth one that was even more efficient. She had looked at several properties, such as density, but had found no significant correlation.

Enlightenment had come to her when she had measured the boiling points: 65 degrees for methanol, 78 degrees for ethanol, and as high as 138 degrees for pentanol. These results seemed to be directly related to the duration she obtained during her tests. It was clear that he needed to create an alcohol with as high a boiling point as possible to achieve better performance.

On her workbench, Marianna had arranged a series of rare ingredients, including a resin extracted from an exotic tree and various essential oils. She decided to distill the resin together with pentanol, hoping that the combination would produce a substance with a higher boiling point. Marianna began by slowly heating the resin and pentanol in a glass still, gradually adding essential oils that acted as catalysts. The reaction required precise control of temperature and pressure to prevent the pentanol from evaporating too soon. Using rudimentary temperature control device, Marianna kept the mix at a constant heat, carefully monitoring each change in the process, she added an alkali metal compound that she had synthesized through a lengthy process of electrolysis. This additive, a combination of potassium and sodium, was known to alter the properties of organic compounds. Her hope was that the additive would bond the molecules of pentanol and resin, creating a new compound with a much higher boiling point.

As the mix continued to heat up, Marianna observed an amazing transformation. The resin and pentanol molecules began to form stronger bonds due to the alkali metal additive.

After several hours of waiting and meticulous adjustments, she noticed that the liquid in the capacitor began to collect into an amber substance with an intense, sweet aroma.

With great excitement, she measured the boiling point of the new compound and discovered that it was an impressive 355 degrees, far higher than that of pentanol. She had created a new type of alcohol, which he named 'Amber Elixir,' in honor of its unique color and properties.

During the experiments of the following days, however, he noticed with disappointment that Elixir did not behave like pentanol in the fuel cell: it seemed that the anode could not break down the alcohol so as to efficiently generate energy. Marianna had tried different catalysts to facilitate the reaction but nothing seemed to work.

It was during a rainy day that enlightenment came to her: she watched the drops of water run down the windowpane and suddenly wondered why the drops had that shape. The round shape must have had some particular advantage in nature for that phenomenon to occur.

Until then he had always used thin-sheet anodes and cathodes, simply because they were the easiest to construct. She decided to try modifying the shape of the electrodes, inspired by that of water droplets. She would then try semi-sphere-shaped cathode and anode.

The result was surprising. With the half-spherical electrodes, the Elixir immediately began to react with oxygen and generate electricity extremely efficiently. larger surface area and optimization of the contact between the Elixir and the electrodes enabled a more efficient reaction, demonstrating that the spherical shape significantly improved the pre-stations of the fuel cell.

A year after her first trial with methanol, Marianna was ready to test the efficiency of Elixir. The result was astounding. With one liter of Elixir and hemispherical electrodes, he could travel nearly 30 nautical miles, a distance 20 times greater than that achieved with methanol. With this efficiency, 350 liters would have been more than enough to travel to and from the United States. However, as she continued testing, Marianna realized new needs. She had to consider a margin for possible loss of cell efficiency, so she told herself that she needed to be able to charge at least 1,000 liters.

In addition, the craft was too visible and would be willing to sacrifice some efficiency to have something less conspicuous, perhaps partially submerged.

Finally, the hemispherical shape of the electrodes took up too much space in a standard craft, requiring a reconsideration of the overall design to optimize the available area.

Once again, nature came to her aid. What for Newton had been an apple, for her was a peach. Biting it, enlightenment came to her: all the energy of the fruit was enclosed between the peel and the stone. Why couldn't it be the same for her craft? She began feverishly calculating the optimal size to meet all the requirements. He realized that he could create an almost spherical craft that would fit the shape of the electrodes and contain the fuel in a cavity along the edge, as the pulp of the peach lies between the peel (the outer part of the craft) and the kernel (which would accommodate provisions and passengers). With some basic math, she calculated that to contain 1,000 liters of fuel in a four-meter-diameter boat, only five inches of cavity would be needed! This solution not only solved the space problem but also allowed for a more compact and efficient design. Her boat would thus be able to sail discreetly (partially submerged), with all the fuel it needed and with a structure optimized for the efficiency of its semi-spherical electrodes.

At that point, Marianna realized that she needed Alessandro's support. Her finances and skills were not sufficient to carry out this ambitious project on her own. Alessandro, with his experience and practical spirit, was the perfect person to turn his calculations and ideas into reality.

Together, they began to work secretly, using as their workshop an old, abandoned shed at the outskirts of the village where Marianna lived. This secluded place was perfect for avoiding prying eyes and ensuring the confidentiality of their work.

The first step was to procure the necessary materials without arousing suspicion. Marianna and Alessandro bought high-quality wood, metals, and other resources from different suppliers, being careful not to attract attention. They also used some of Alessandro's personal funds, saved over the years, to buy the specialized tools they needed.

Alessandro worked on the structure of the craft, using the precise measurements calculated by Marianna. He created a sturdy spherical skeleton, adapting its shape to include the cavity needed to hold the Elixir. Marianna, meanwhile, devoted himself to fine-tuning the hemispherical electrodes, improving their design to maximize their efficiency.

The nights were long and the days tiring, but both were determined. They worked late into the night, taking advantage of every available moment to advance their project. The shed was lit only by a few oil lamps, casting dancing shadows on the walls as Marianna and Alessandro moved with precision and concentration.

In the end, to minimize water resistance, they had opted for a diameter of five meters and a height of three meters. The upper part of the boat was constructed of wood, chosen for its lightness and ease of workability, while the lower part was made of copper.

The wood of the upper part had been treated with a combination of oils and tar, a traditional technique used to protect ships from water. These materials, which were readily available, provided good waterproofing and resistance to weathering. Alessandro had suggested the use of copper for the bottom after observing that many ships of the time used this metal to protect their hulls from the corrosive action of salt water and the adhesion of marine organisms. Copper also conferred greater structural strength, which was essential for the pressures experienced by the bottom of the boat.

Marianna and Alessandro worked with meticulous attention, integrating the copper and wood into a harmonious structure.

The joints between the two materials were carefully sealed using natural resin and pitch mastic to prevent water while ensuring an optimal hydrodynamic surface. The smooth, continuous curves of the boat were designed to minimize turbulence and improve the efficiency of movement through the water.

When completed, the boat presented a rugged yet elegant appearance, ready to challenge the waves and demonstrate the effectiveness of Elixir as a power source. The combination of wood and copper, in addition to meeting technical requirements, gave the boat a unique character, symbolizing the perfect fusion of innovation and tradition.

After months of relentless work, the craft began to take shape. Each piece of the puzzle fit perfectly: the spherical structure, the hemispherical electrodes, and the gap for the fuel. Their creation was ready to be tested. With their hearts pounding with excitement, they took the boat to a safe place near the coast. At dawn, when the sea was still calm and deserted, they put their work to the test, Marianna at the helm and Alessandro as passenger. The boat glided over the water, almost silent; Marianna and Alessandro smiled, knowing they had accomplished something extraordinary.

Everything, then, continued for the best, at least until that day.

Alessandro had now lost all faith in the new French governesses, who seemed interested in science only when it had warlike applications. He did not want the Elixir and the Peach (that is what they had named their craft) to fall into their hands. Even Marianna understood that they might have to get rid of that invention to prevent it from being exploited for military purposes.

She did not want to destroy her work but saw no alternative in that he could not escape: the French had a dominant presence in much of the known world, and with their American allies they were also present in the New World. Escape seemed impossible.

Alessandro, however, suggested a solution. "South America is under control of Spain. You could find refuge there," he said. Although Spain was allied with France through the Treaty of San

Ildefonso, the vast territory and local autonomy offered by the South American colonies could provide a safe place for Marianna to continue her work without French interference.

Marianna hesitated. "But how can I reach South America without being discovered? What about you, Alessandro?"

Alessandro answered with determination, "You have to go alone. I am too visible and suspicious for the French authorities. I have to stay here and pretend I don't know anything. With the Peach, you will be able to navigate discreetly and avoid the main routes. It's risky but it's the best chance."

Then he added, "I have a contact in Argentina, an old family friend who can help you. His name is Miguel Ferrero, he is an important industrialist in Buenos Aires. I'll write a letter of introduction in which I'll mention your situation; show it to him when you arrive and I'm sure he'll protect you."

Marianna sounded unconvinced: "Do you think he will trust a stranger who shows up with a letter with probably not very credible content?"

Alessandro thought about it for a moment and then replied, "The only alternative would be to have a letter of mine given by a different person anticipate your arrival, that way your arrival will be pre-announced and the risks of not being believed will be much less. You must leave right away, though; there is no way this letter will get to Argentina before you do."

"Unless I make a stop at a safe place during the journey. The Peach is spacious, I can load all the supplies I want," Marianna replied.

Alessandro did two calculations in his mind, "In mid-November a ship will leave Genoa for Buenos Aires. I could give the letter to their captain and you an uncommon object for Miguel to identify you without a doubt. Calculating the speed of the Peach compared to traditional sailing vessels, you will have to wait about four weeks during the voyage so that you can be sure the letter will arrive you do. Are you up for it?"

Marianna felt a glimmer of hope. "Thank you, Alessandro. I don't know what I'll do without you, but I'll do my best." Alessandro squeezed her hands, looking into her eyes. "I know you will make it, Marianna. You are one of the most intelligent and courageous people I know. Now, we must act in hurry."

The next day, Alessandro showed up at the De Mar Hotel, where he knew the captain of the boat bound for Buenos Aires resided. The captain, a stout man with a thick black beard and piercing eyes, was sitting at the hotel bar, sipping a glass of rum.

"Captain Leclerc, good evening," said Alessandro approaching with a smile. The captain recognized him immediately and stood up to shake his hand.

"Good evening, Volta. It's always nice to meet you," he replied in a deep, warm voice. "To what do I owe the pleasure of your visit?"

"I have a special request, captain," Alessandro began, taking a sealed envelope from the inside pocket of his coat. "I have to ask you a favor of great importance. This envelope must be delivered in Buenos Aires, to a man named Miguel Ferrero. He is the owner of one of the largest textile factories in the city."

Leclerc took the envelope carefully, looking at it attentively. "Miguel Ferrero, owner of the textile factory. I see. And what's in this envelope, if you don't mind me asking?"

"This is a very delicate business matter," replied Alessandro, lowering his voice. "Please make sure he receives it personally. You will arrive in Buenos Aires at the end of December, when it is midsummer there. It is crucial that Ferrero receives this information without any delay."

The captain nodded, putting the envelope in the inside pocket of his coat. "You can count on me, Volta. I will make sure the envelope reaches its destination. And don't worry, we loaded the ship with valuable goods for Buenos Aires: fine fabrics, weapons, and exotic spices. The journey will be long, but we are well prepared."

Alessandro visibly relaxed, knowing that he could continue to rely on the captain's reliability. "Thank you, Leclerc. I know I can trust you. This envelope contains information that could make a difference to many."

The captain smiled, clapping a hand on the shoulder of

Alessandro. "Don't worry, my friend. I will see to it that Miguel Ferrero receives the envelope. Now, give yourself some rest. You look like you need it."

"Thank you, captain. I will," Alessandro said with a tired but grateful smile. "Have a safe journey and good luck." "And to you, Volta. I'll see you on our return," replied the captain, raising his glass in salute. Alessandro did the same, feeling a weightlift from his shoulders as he left the hotel, certain that the message would arrive to its destination.

Dear Miguel,

I hope this letter finds you in good health. It has been a long time since we last saw each other, but I remember fondly the times we spent together and our friendship that endured the years and distance.

I am writing to you with an urgent and personal request. A woman named Marianna Paris will present herself to you. She is a dear colleague of mine and someone I trust deeply. Marianna will show you an Italian flag (or rather, what will hopefully become the flag of Italy in the future: it is similar to the French flag but with green instead of blue) on which I will write her name, as proof of our connection.

Please protect her and provide her with all the help she needs until I can contact you again. The circumstances that brought her there are extremely delicate and her safety is vitally important.

I know I can count on you, Miguel, as I have so many times in the past. Marianna is involved in a very important and risky project and her presence in Buenos Aires must remain discreet and protected. I appreciate your assistance in this matter immensely and I am sure you understand the gravity of the situation.

As soon as circumstances permit, I will contact you for further instructions. In the meantime, I ask that you treat Marianna as you would a member of your family.

With gratitude and affection, Alessandro Volta

He had not noticed that seconds after him, Charles Moreau had entered the bar and sat at a small table in the shade, watching them.

OFF THE COAST OF CHILE

January, 1803 I think

I finally managed to stop Peach, get some fresh air and have enough light to be able to update this journal. The last days have been terrifying; I don't know how I made it out alive. The performance of the Peach's engine and power supply is evidently superior to what I myself thought, able to make up for the less- than-state-of-the-art navigation system.

The trip to Argentina went incredibly well; I think it took me only a month, not counting the weeks stopover in Africa. The sea was always calm and no one saw me, not even when I crossed, at night, the Strait of Gibraltar.

The explanations and tools Alessandro had provided me with to orient myself, along with the fact that, with the Peach, I do not have to follow the winds, allowed me to quickly cross the Atlantic and skirt Brazil without any problems.

When I was a short time away from arriving, almost in the Bay of Buenos Aires, all hell broke. It was late in the evening but evidently they saw me and started shooting at me with cannons! I was able to lean out to look to see if they were really firing at me or I had perhaps accidentally passed in the middle of a naval clash but I saw three French brigs lined up firing directly at me.

They were waiting for me, it was obvious! They must have discovered my destination and sent as many as three brigs to wait for me. They must have sensed the real potential of my vessel to deploy so many forces.

I wonder how they found out my destination. The only explanation I can think of is that they have intercepted Alessandro's letter to Miguel, but this means Alessandro may also be in danger! I try to reassure myself by thinking that the French must have already guessed that he was connected to me and the boat, but they must have realized that he was not aware of the technical details, otherwise they would have questioned him well before my departure. After the naval collision I was able to quickly change course and head south. I think I reached Cape Horn in terrible conditions. For two days the waves were so big that I couldn't move, but the Peach, thanks its closed shape, is unsinkable. There the brigs could not chase me.

As soon as the sea calmed down, I was able to leave again. I still got plenty of provisions, water and Elixir.

I can no longer go back to Buenos Aires, partly because I don't want to go through Cape Horn hell again.

I will go north and rely on fate.

BERGAMO, ITALY

Tuesday, January 22, 2019

In the office, Gabriele just could not concentrate. He struggled to remember that his salary, and thus his livelihood, basically depended on correctly entering numbers into Excel. For a moment he smiled at this thought, finding something distorted about it. It was strange to think that pressing keys on a pc in a certain order his survival any more than jobs where physical or technical skills were crucial would.

He thought, for example, of the operators in his company who repaired machinery, equipment he could hardly even identify, and who probably had lower salaries and corporate security than he did.

Rationally, he answered himself that the way he and his colleagues entered those numbers into Excel depended on the acquisition of new business for the company and, consequently, also on the jobs and economic security of those workers. However, irrationally, it still seemed strange to him and he kept thanking his luck and his parents who had given him the opportunity to pursue that career path. That morning, however, entering those numbers was the least of his problems. He had not slept at night, thinking about the voyage of the spherical vessel from Genoa to Ibaraki.

Setting out in the second half of 1802, he had calculated that the vessel would have to travel about 20,000 miles to reach its destination. The journey would begin by crossing the Mediterranean and passing through Gibraltar, a heavily defended British outpost that was strategically vital in the frequent wars between England and France. Gibraltar was a crucial point for controlling the sea routes between the Atlantic and the Mediterranean, with its strong fortifications and the constant presence of the Royal Navy.

Having crossed the Atlantic, the vessel would coast across South America to the Strait of Magellan or Cape Horn, one of the most dangerous areas in the world: with its treacherous waters and stormy winds, it posed a formidable challenge to navigators.

Past the southern tip of South America, the route would probably have led between Easter Island, discovered only not so many years earlier by Dutchman Jakob Roggeveen, and the coast of Chile, which at that time was still completely under Spanish control.

Navigation would then continue south of Hawaii, under the rule of the legendary King Kamehameha I, who at that time was consolidating his control over the Hawaiian Islands, unifying the archipelago under his reign through military prowess and strategic alliances.

Finally, the vessel would land in February 1803 on the bare beaches of Ibaraki, in a Japan still under the isolationist sakoku policy, which severely restricted contact with foreigners.

The vessel had certainly been seen in Genoa before departure (he had the French maritime police report to prove it) but he had found no more references to the spherical ship in the French records of the period. During the rest of the voyage, it could have been sighted in Gibraltar by British forces, in Brazil by Portuguese forces, or in Argentina by Spanish forces. He would hardly have found written accounts regarding passage near Easter Island or Hawaii. Finally, the United States still had no presence on the West Coast at that time, considering that Lewis and Clark's famous explorations did not begin until 1804. There was, however, that strange reference to the 'American government' found by Luna in Choshi. Until late into the night, he had done Google searches such as 'spherical boat Brazil,' 'Genoa Japan voyage 1800,' 'Gibraltar Naval Records 1800' and, of course, had not found anything.

He did not want to give Luna only the report from the Genoa police; he hoped to be able to provide her with something more concrete. However, random Google searches would not have led to anything significant. If information of that magnitude had really been available, it would have already been in the public domain.

The only archive where he could find interesting news was the one Marie had given him access to. The day seemed never to pass. Even his colleagues, seeing his dreamy air during lunch, asked him if there was anything wrong but Gabriele always answered evasively. He was looking forward to going home.

He went out as quickly as possible and by 6 p.m. he was already in front of the PC with login credentials entered. Given that the only source of information could be the French archives, he focused on new research starting with what he had already found. He remembered a reference made by Captain François Dupont, who had suggested proceeding with a more thorough investigation of what he believed to be, rather than a sea creature, a peculiar and potentially dangerous vessel.

He changed the time limits of the search, moving it to 1830 to make sure he did not miss anything, and entered 'Capitaine François Dupont' as the search parameter. Sixty-three results appeared, and Gabriele felt almost overwhelmed at the idea of having to translate and read 63 potentially tedious documents. He knew, however, that this was the only way he could hope to make a significant breakthrough in the search and give Luna the information she desired.

Today, January 7, 1800, at 08:30 a.m., a maritime accident occurred in front of the port of Genoa. The merchant ship La Belle Étoile, under the command of Captain Jean-Luc Lemoine, suffered severe damage from a sudden storm.

As the ship approached the harbor, an exceptionally powerful wave struck its port side, causing it to tilt sharply and causing significant damage to the hull. The reduced visibility and sea conditions made it impossible to properly maneuver the ship to avoid the accident.

During the accident, several cargo crates were moved and some fell overboard, causing a considerable loss of cargo. In addition, deckhand Dominique Leclerc was injured by one of the crates coming loose from its supports. He was immediately rescued by the crew and later transported to the local infirmary to receive necessary medical treatment.

After inspecting the ship and assessing the damage, it was considered that the hull needs urgent repairs. Captain Lemoine has already contacted the Genoa shipyard to organize the necessary repairs to ensure the safety of the ship.

The crew showed great competence and courage in handling the emergency, and no additional injuries were reported among crew members or passengers.

This report will be forwarded to the appropriate authorities for further action and verification.

Signed,

Capitaine François Dupont Maritime Police of Genoa

Nothing of interest.

He moved on to the second, then the third document, and realized that he could not continue that way. He was about to close the search when he noticed something strange: of the 63 documents, 18 were from 1800, 23 from 1801, and 22 from 1802. None of the documents were after September 23, 1802. Had he perhaps found the date of the captain's death? It could have made sense: maybe he had uncovered a plot related to the spherical ship and had been assassinated by some secret agency! He said to himself that if he was making those arguments, maybe it was time to go to sleep but he felt he was on the right track and had to continue. It was now 10 o'clock in the evening. He drank a glass of water, refreshed his face and sat back down at the computer.

He googled information about the military organization of the French army in the 19th century and found that the next role after Capitaine was Commandant.

He returned to the French document archive and searched for 'Commandant François Dupont'. Great!

41 documents, the first of which is dated February 1803. So, François had been promoted between the fall of 1802 and the winter of 1803.

He read a couple of them. François was now living in Paris at the Bureau de la Police Générale. He quickly inquired and discovered that this bureau, under Joseph Fouché, Minister of Police, was responsible for internal security and intelligence gathering.

Basically, a spy agency. The connection between his move to the secret police and the discovery and initial investigation of the spherical craft could have been more than a coincidence.

The nature of the documents had changed radically. They were no longer minutes of trivial incidents but transcripts of letters, reports of meetings and gatherings. He did not know what to expect but sensed that they might conceal crucial information.

The reasoning that relevant documents would already have been filed by other researchers still applied; all the while, he was aware that at this point he had to read them all. If there was a connection between Dupont and the Utsuro Bune, these documents might hold the key to unlocking it.

'*Date: 15 June 1803 Location: Paris*

Participants: Général Pierre Leclerc, Commandant François Dupont

Général Leclerc: Commandant Dupont, thank you for coming. We have received disturbing reports about possible Austrian infiltration of our administration in Milan. It is essential that we address this threat with the utmost urgency.

Commandant Dupont: I understand, Général. What is the evidence we have so far?

Général Leclerc: Several intercepted communications indicate that the Austrians are trying to destabilize our presence in Milan. They have established contacts with some local elements opposed to our control. We have also noticed suspicious movements in the vicinity of the Royal Palace.

Commandant Dupont: What measures do you suggest we take, Général?

Général Leclerc: We need to launch a thorough investigation. I would like you to organize a trusted team to monitor suspicious individuals. We will have to use both plainclothes and military officers to ensure maximum effectiveness.

Commandant Dupont: It will be done, Général. I will make sure that every movement is documented and that any evidence is carefully collected and analyzed.

Général Leclerc: Perfect, Dupont. It is vital that this operation remains confidential. We cannot allow our intentions to be discovered. The safety of our work in Milan depends on the success of this mission.

Commandant Dupont: Understood, Général. I will begin preparations immediately.

Général Leclerc: Well, we are counting on you, Dupont. Our position in northern Italy must remain firm and unchallenged.

Signed,

Général Pierre Leclerc, Commandant François Dupont'

Gabriele read several minutes and letters of the same tone. Each one was increasingly tiring to read both because of little interest and the increasingly late hours.

'June 23, 1803 Major John Kendrick,

I would like to thank you for your assistance and support of our cause. Your cooperation has been of great importance to our research, and we trust that your efforts will continue to bear fruit.

The information we seek could have a significant impact on relations between our two nations. It is essential that your efforts translate into concrete results.

As you prepare for your next voyage on the Lady Washington, know that the success of your mission is of utmost importance. Your experience and determination are admirable, but now is the time to demonstrate your ability to complete tasks of crucial strategic importance.

We appreciate your contribution so far but look forward to the results of your research. We are confident that you will understand the urgency and sensitivity of the situation.

With respect and determination, Commandant François Dupont'

Boy, this guy Kendrick had gotten a good earful in the style of 'Efforts are appreciated, results are rewarded'.

He continued like this for three more papers but finally decided to stop. It was 1 a.m. and the next day he would have to go to the office at the usual time. He got up from his chair and put on his pajamas but a strange feeling buzzed in his head. Had he overlooked something? It seemed to him that he had glimpsed a shadow in his thoughts, one of those fleeting insights that fade away like dreams in the morning.

He went to bed but that feeling continued to torment him. After a few minutes of agitation, gave up. He got up and went back to the PC with the intention of rereading all the documents he had saved. There was no need to read them all, however. When he saw the names 'John Kendrick' and 'Lady Washington,' something clicked in his mind. He remembered that Kendrick had been the first commander and the Lady Washington the first American vessel to approach Japan in the early 1800s.

Adrenaline took over, and he realized that he could no longer sleep.

IBARAKI, JAPAN

Wednesday, January 23, 2019

Luna was at her most excited. It was all true. Gabriele, as usual, had found a way to make it up to her, and what a way!

He had telephoned her early in the morning, late at night in Italy, and passed her information that virtually completed the picture. There was documentary evidence showing that a spherical ship had been sighted off Genoa in the spring of 1802 by a certain Captain François Dupont. This captain had initiated an investigation and had been promoted to Commandant and transferred to Paris, in the secret police.

In 1803, Dupont had contacted U.S. marine major John Kendrick for important research for France to the point that could change the relationship between the two countries. Kendrick, posing as a merchant, had been Japan's first non-incidental visitor aboard the Lady Washington.

A few months before the meeting between Dupont and Kendrick, the spherical vessel had arrived in Ibaraki with a red-haired woman inside and an Italian flag bearing the name Marianna Paris, former mistress of Alessandro Volta, one of the most brilliant minds in history. Thus, up to 1807, the Tokugawa government had been pressuring the rulers of Ibaraki, the Satake clan, to find information about the landing, evidently under the military threat of Kendrick, a mi- ness that would be realized a couple of decades later with the arrival of Commodore Perry.

It was all incredible. The historical connections, the international plots, and the central role of Marianna Paris in the context. Luna felt overwhelmed with adrenaline and the awareness that she was one step closer to the truth.

As soon as she had received this information from Gabriele, she had not been able to understand how facts of such magnitude could have remained hidden for so long, but as she re-read the French documents, she realized that, outside of the context, they carried no relevant information. Only the connection between spherical craft, Captain Dupont and the Lady Washington had made those two documents so important to their research.

For the past few days her boss, Kato-san, had been acting strangely. She had heard from him only once on the telephone and then nothing more. His very strong interest in research seemed to have waned. However, Luna was certain that everything would change as soon as she brought him the new documents.

Before going to Kato, she decided to return to Ibaraki to Kiyoshi. It had all started from his library and she felt it was her duty update him first. Next, she would pay a visit to Ito-san, who had phoned her asking for updates and offering to help with anything. He had been very kind and helpful.

For the past few days, she had been staying at her mom and Emi's house. Kato-san had told her to devote herself exclusively to research, and suddenly she had stopped checking in, a sign that she was not needed in the library. This gave her the freedom to manage her time as she preferred.

She had, of course, updated Emi on the progress achieved thanks to Gabriele, showing her the PDFs of the two key documents she had received by email. She had also asked her to take care of Mom as usual, making sure that everything was under control while she continued her mission.

She headed to the station for the long train ride. This time she would not take the usual route via Tokyo but would travel north, with a change Oyama, Tochigi Prefecture. Perhaps the trip would have taken a little longer, but she wished to avoid the chaos of the capital.

Considering that her appointment with Kiyoshi was at 4 p.m., she decided to stop in Oyama for lunch. The town was renowned for yuba, a delicious tofu skin that she loved to eat fried along with a plate of sushi.

The train glided through bucolic landscapes, and Luna felt relaxed, knowing that she had plenty of time. Arriving in Oyama, she found a small traditional restaurant and ordered her favorite dish. The fried yuba was crispy and flavorful, perfect for recharging herself before continuing the journey.

After a satisfying lunch, complete with a ritual plate photo and a short walk around the city, she resumed the train and arrived at the Ibaraki Prefectural Museum on time for her appointment with Kiyoshi.

Kiyoshi greeted her at the museum gate with a warm smile. He looked dapper in a suit and tie, which his distinguished features and handsome athletic physique.

"Hello Luna-chan," he greeted her. "I'm sorry again for the little time I was able to give you last time, I'm glad you're back."

"Hello Kiyoshi-san," Luna replied, "thank you for your helpfulness. I would never have made all these discoveries without your help!"

"You must tell me everything," Kiyoshi said, "but let's go to my office and talk calmly."

Kiyoshi's office was not in the main building as Luna expected, but in the basement of a secondary hall. It was still bright and spacious, a bit bare, with only plastic chairs and a modest desk without a computer.

"Are you surprised by my office? This is the quietest place in the whole museum, and here I can stand among the books without anyone disturbing me unless it is strictly necessary," Kiyoshi said, noticing Luna's curious look.

"I completely understand, in a museum peace of mind is fundamental," Luna replied.

"Have a seat and tell me everything you have discovered," Kiyoshi invited her, pointing to one of the plastic chairs.

Luna sat down and began to narrate, feeling at ease in that serene environment, surrounded by books and Kiyoshi's company.

"Kiyoshi-san," Luna began, with sudden haste in her voice, "you can't imagine! Gabriele found evidence that the French and American governments were looking for the Utsuro Bune!"

Kiyoshi was silent for a moment, then asked, "The Utsuro Bune? Meaning?"

"Look here!" Luna stood up and went next to him, showing him the two documents from Gabriele that she had printed on paper. "The U.S. Navy pressured the Tokugawa to help them discover the truth about the Utsuro Bune. They and France understood the potential of that invention. The Tokugawa were probably cornered by some military threat and were forced to conduct investigations through the Satake clan. The Satake clan got no results and perhaps this created initial friction with the United States, which then probably contributed to Commodore Perry's action and, as a consequence, the fall of the Shoguns!"

Luna had spoken all once, with the smile of someone who is discovering historical truths that have come to light after more than two hundred years.

Seeing Kiyoshi's thoughtful expression, she added to lighten the tension, "Think how bad it looks for the Satake clan: for their inability to do research they could practically be held responsible for the fall of the Shoguns." She smiled. Kiyoshi, who had been silent the whole time looking at the documents, shifted his gaze to her. It was a cold look.

He stood up and stood in front of Luna.

"Kiyoshi-san, what is it? You make me uncomfortable," Luna said with a veil of concern.

Suddenly, Kiyoshi pushed her with both hands, causing her to take a step back and exclaimed in a low, threatening voice, "It's not the Satake clan's fault! They've been betrayed by their own people, by that damned Shoya who hid essential information!"

"Kiyoshi-san, what are you doing?" Luna was now afraid. Kiyoshi advanced another step and pushed her back again violently. "Because of this event, the Satake clan has fallen into disgrace! Only the finding of the Utsuro Bune by a clan member can bring it back the glory it deserves." Now Kiyoshi's eyes were red; he seemed delirious.

"Kiyoshi-san! What are you talking about? What do you know?"

"Luna, what's my last name?" asked Kiyoshi with a sneer.

"Sakubu..." replied Luna, more confused than afraid.

Kiyoshi remained silent, looked at her questioningly with a

slight smile, and waited for Luna to come to her own conclusion.
So, Luna understood, "Sakubu's kanji, they can also be read as..."
she paused.

Kiyoshi finished the sentence, "Like Satake. That's right! I am a
direct descendant of the Satake clan. We had to change our last
name to Sakubu because of the dishonor caused by the Utsuro
Bune. I came specifically to Ibaraki to continue the search. What
do you think an Italian flag was doing in a binder on Tax and
Revenue? Do you think we are so messy? I put it there when I
heard you were coming! A fresh mind could have brought some
new information."

The puzzle pieces were finally finding their places in Luna's
head.

"You did well in deciphering the record of Choshi's interrogation,
but we had already done that too. You were supposed to find
more information about the boat's hiding place, not meddle in
political issues that must stay buried forever!"

Luna retreated farther and farther back, but Kiyoshi was
constantly a step away from her, until she felt her back against
the wall.

"That John Kendrick and his Lady Washington were to be lost
in history. The first Americans who dared to come close to
Japan... With his cannons and muskets, he set the coast of
Ibaraki on fire. The Tokugawa were terrified; they would have
done anything to send him away. They forced my clan into an
impossible quest. My ancestors tried everything but could not
satisfy the Tokugawa and the Americans. The Satake clan was
then dispersed and the Americans came back more and more
aggressively, until Perry and his black ships arrived..."

Kiyoshi continued, "How did you find out about the connection?
We thought we had hidden all the evidences! Oh, it doesn't
matter anyway. I was right to bring you to this dirty closet. Oh!
Did you really think it was my office?" He burst into sinister
laughter. "Here no one can hear you, and here you will stay until I
complete my research!" Kiyoshi, now completely beside himself,
gave her one last loud shove that caused her to slam violently

against the wall.

Luna felt an excruciating pain in the back of her head, slumped to the ground, and, before everything went black, had time for one last thought about the sentence Kiyoshi had spoken: 'You were supposed to find more information about the boat's hiding place'.

Kiyoshi knew, the Utsuro Bune was in Japan.

BERGAMO, ITALY

Friday, January 25, 2019

Gabriele usually set three alarm clocks in the morning so that he could get up: the first one warned him that he would have to get up shortly, the second one told him that the time had arrived, and the third one prompted him, well knowing that the second one had been ignored. Between the first and second wake-up calls, there came a phone call via WhatsApp.

With half an eye open, he looked at the name of the person who was calling him.

"Emi-chan?!" he exclaimed. Why Luna's sister contacting him? He replied worriedly, "Moshi moshi Emi-chan, genki?"

Emi replied in English, "Hi Gabriele-kun, sorry to tell you-. I'm fine but I'm worried."

"What's going on?"

"I can't find Luna. Two days ago she went to Ibaraki to talk to Kiyoshi-san from Utsuro Bune but I haven't heard from her since and her cell phone is reported to be turned off." Emi's voice was distressed, bordering on tears.

"Did you call the police?" asked Gabriele alarmed. Two days of disappearance could mean something serious.

"Yes, but they don't seem too worried: as an adult, she is free to do whatever she wants, they don't have to look for all the people who don't answer their cell phones right away," spied Emi, "But we were supposed to talk on Wednesday night and instead the cell phone has been off since then."

Gabriele agreed, something could have happened. But how could he help? He certainly could not go to Japan and set out to find her....

"She was supposed to meet with Kiyoshi, right?" asked Gabriele.

"Yes, I called him yesterday but he said Luna did not get to him. He tried to call her after half an hour after the appointment time but found his cell phone turned off. Then he didn't think any more about it."

Gabriele thought about how to at least find the area where she could be.

"Emi-chan, do you have his Google account password?"

"If he hasn't changed it lately, yes."

"Call me on the PC via Skype that we'll give it a try." Five minutes later, they were connected on Skype with Emi sharing her screen.

They had managed to Luna's Google account, and Gabriele asked to see her Google Maps history. The last search was for the best route from Oyama to the Prefectural Museum of Ibaraki, made at 1 p.m. on Wednesday.

Gabriele smiled for a moment: she had stopped in Oyama, surely to eat fried yuba.

This thought moved him and increased his urgency in his research.

"That doesn't give us any information, we already knew she was going to Ibaraki," Gabriele said. "Let's try Google Photo, see the last picture she took and if it tells us where she was."

Emi showed the last photo taken: a plate of fried yuba with sushi. Of course.

He couldn't think of any other application that could record the location. There was 'Find My iPhone,' but Emi had already said that she had not activated the function on his phone to search for Luna's.

One last idea came to Gabriele.

"Luna-chan used Google Fit if I remember correctly," he said. Emi did a quick check. "Yes, it is active but doesn't register the last position."

"What is last physical activity she did?"

"2.9 miles, 44 minutes, 2 flights of stairs," Emi replied. Gabriele quickly opened Google Maps. Distance between Mito Station and Prefectural Museum of Ibaraki:

2.8 miles, 39 minutes.

"Emi!" exclaimed Gabriele urgently, even forgetting the chan suffix. "Luna arrived at the museum and even went up two flights of stairs there! Kiyoshi may be lying!"

"And why should it?" asked Emi increasingly alarmed. "And what can I do? Do I tell the police?"

Gabriele was silent for a moment. He had Luna in front of him, taking the picture of the yuba dish, happy, thinking about what was ahead of her; he thought how stupid they had been to make that decision in the April of 2018, how he had been trying to deny that he was still in love with her for the past few months, the fact that the closing day of the Ibaraki Museum was Monday and so he would have the whole weekend to look for traces Luna there.

"Yes, tell it to the police," said Gabriele. "Anyway, I'm coming. Tomorrow night I will be in Ibaraki."

TOKYO, JAPAN

Saturday, April 14, 2018

Luna and Gabriele, backpacking, had just boarded the Joban Line train that would take them to the Tsuchiura station, north of Chiba. From there they would take a bus for a fifty-miles ride their destination, Mount Tsukuba. Luna had suggested that they take advantage of the first warm day for a walk in the mountains, and at dawn they were off.

Luna, experienced and forward-thinking, wore a technical outfit perfect for the hike. Her lightweight but waterproof windbreaker jacket in a vibrant turquoise color was paired with hiking pants with many pockets, ideal for storing small items. Her hiking shoes were sturdy and well- used, a sign of his many past adventures. Underneath her jacket, she wore a breathable long-sleeved T-shirt and a fleece mid-layer that kept her warm without making her sweat. She also had a hat with a visor to protect her from the sun and a compact but roomy backpack containing a water bottle, some energy snacks, and a route map. Gabriele, on the other hand, was clearly showing his inexperience. He was wearing jeans, definitely unsuitable for an excursion, and a heavy sweatshirt that, although comfortable, was neither breathable nor suitable for temperature changes. On his feet, he wore old sneakers, which certainly did not offer the right support or traction for mountain trails. His backpack was a sports bag more suited to the gym than the mountains, and he had not thought to carry a hat or a light second layer. Despite his good will, Gabriele appeared clumsy, making Luna smile at the obvious contrast between the two.

They had been engaged for almost two years and were very happy together. They seemed made for each other. They shared similar rhythms, could spend hours in silence or chatting nonstop, teasing each other and fighting only over silly things. Luna had gone through some very bad times after her parents' accident about a year before but Gabriele had always been there for her and had supported her when she needed it most.

It seemed like a dream story but there was always a shadow looming over them, a shadow they both knew but never named. That was why Luna had not moved in with Gabriele, and he had never insisted on the move. Certainly, they practically lived together on weekends and she had her own toothbrush and pajamas in Hiroo's nice apartment, but it was different.

For two years they had avoided addressing the issue, but by now it was only a few months away and they would have to make a decision that neither of them wanted to make but for which neither of them saw an alternative.

After an hour and fifteen minutes by train through the Chiba fields, they arrived at their first stop, the small town of Tsuchiura. The town was located on the shore of the large Lake Kasumigaura, the second largest lake in Japan. The shores of the lake were bordered by lush vegetation, with cherry trees, maritime pines, and reeds dancing to the rhythm of light breezes.

In the mid-morning spring light, the sun painted the water with golden and orange hues, while fishing boats moved slowly, creating gentle waves on the calm surface. Local fishermen, experienced and patient, cast their nets to nab a few eels, while waterfowl glided elegantly, seeking their meal.

Gabriele hardly restrained himself from suggesting to Luna that we take a walk along the wooden walkways that went into the waters of Kasumigaura, imagining that it could be an experience of absolute peace.

Once on the bus, Luna explained the day's program in more detail. "Do you see this temple on the map?"

"The Tsukubasan?" asked Gabriele.

"That's right. We get off at this stop, then follow this path all the way to the top," Luna explained, pointing with her finger to a thin green line that snaked down the mountain.

"The Sakurazaka trail on Mount Tsukuba is really beautiful," Luna began. "It starts at the foot of the mountain and the trail winds through a landscape full of cherry trees. In spring, cherry blossoms explode everywhere in pink and white, it's a sight. The peak of the bloom has passed but perhaps, toward the top, where it is colder, there may be more. The trail is well maintained, with paved sections and stone steps, so it is easy to walk. Along the way, are small streams running through the path, and the sound of flowing water is really relaxing. There are also wooden benches and rest areas where we can stop to rest and admire the view. A kaleidoscope of colors."

Gabriele burst out laughing, "Kaleidoscope? Are you trying to use a word you just learned?"

Luna also laughed. "Exactly. But let me continue! From some vantage points," he continued, "you can see the plains below and, on a clear day, even the Pacific Ocean in the distance. It's really spectacular, especially in autumn, when the leaves of the trees turn red and orange."

She realized too late that she had referred to the autumn, moment when they would no longer be together. No more, she had to close the topic. Today was the day to address this taboo. But not now. She quickly resumed speaking.

"As we approach the summit, the trail becomes steeper, but it is worth it. From the top, with the twin peaks Nantai and Nyotai, you have an incredible panoramic view. You can see the surrounding mountains, the urban expanses of Tokyo and, if we're lucky, even Mount Fuji in the distance."

Gabriele listened fascinated and concerned: Luna had not mentioned the length of the walk...

"We'll have lunch at the top," Luna continued, and Gabriele shaved: assuming we start the hike at 10 a.m., it would last no more than three hours, "and afterwards we'll descend using the funicular to Mount Tsukuba from which we can see forests, chasms, immense rice fields, and, as we face east, we'll also be able to see the ocean. That side of the mountain is also special because there are many statues of frogs."

"How come? Are there lakes full of frogs?" asked Gabriele.

"Absolutely not," Luna replied. "According to a legend, Mount Tsukuba is the home place of a giant frog. This belief is so deeply rooted that visitors to Mount Tsukuba often see frog statues as symbols good luck and protection for travelers. The statues, some as old as hundreds of years, are scattered along route, especially near temples and shrines, and are a tribute to the legend and a sign of good auspiciousness for all the people who visit the mountain."

"But if we go down the other side of the mountain, how do we get back to where we got off the bus?" asked Gabriele. "See here?" replied Luna, pointing to a 'P' on the map. "This is the terminus of the bus. We will take it from here and we'll do the route backwards."

"Great!" concluded Gabriele, reassured.

Four hours later, only a few minutes later than Gabriele had calculated, they were at the Nantai summit observatory. Ahead of them was a spectacular view of all of Tokyo and, in the distance, the majestic Mount Fuji. Seated at a table, they were enjoying curry and its warm, spicy flavor mingling with the freshness of the mountain air.

Gabriele turned back to Luna. The thought of having to say what they could no longer delay squeezed his heart.

"Luna..." he said in a low voice.

"Gabriele..." replied Luna, in the same tone. She too knew that moment was inevitable.

"In five months I'm going back to Italy. I have no choice. The company, by its own policy, has to rotate personnel. During these years I have not been my own master. I depend in everything on Automitalia: the job, the apartment, the visa to stay in Japan..."

"I know," Luna replied.

Gabriele paused and lowered his gaze. "I could ask to stay another six months, maybe a year; they are very willing and would probably accept but then I would still have to leave Japan. I have no long-term future here." After a moment of silence, he added, "Are you coming too?"

Luna gave a bitter smile. "Are you asking me to come live with you in Italy because the company is forcing you to come back?

Thank you for the thought!" Then she continued in a softer tone, "You know with my family situation it would be impossible. My dad left us recently, my mom is in a wheelchair, Emi-chan has to graduate in engineering. I have to stay and help them."

"So?" asked Gabriel, his eyes still on the ground.

"What do you expect, to be able to continue a relationship ten-thousand miles away? And then what do we do, meet for ice cream? Maybe in Dubai? Okay, I'll say it: our relationship will end when you get on that plane."

As predicted by both of them, their relationship ended that day instead. But that reality was too painful to be put into words at that time.

IBARAKI, JAPAN

Saturday, January 26, 2019

As in the worst romantic movies, Gabriele had opened the SkyScanner application while packing a backpack for the trip and saw that a flight to Helsinki was leaving Linate at midday. From there, fifty-five minutes later, the plane to Narita would leave. Fifty-five-minute layovers were really at the limit of possibility but the only alternative available, via Paris, involved a three-hour layover and the arrival was at Haneda, much farther than Narita from Ibaraki. All things considered, passing through Paris certainly would not get to the museum before closing time on Saturday while, passing through Helsinki, he had some chance of being at the museum as early as Saturday afternoon. He was lucky: the flight from Linate left on time and in Helsinki he did not have to go through baggage control but only passport control, so he arrived on time at the boarding gate for Narita.

Once he took off, all the excitement about the sudden journey slipped away and revealed the feeling of panic that had been hidden until then. The girl he was in love with had disappeared, the police were looking for her without too much effort, and perhaps a madman had done something to her.

If he had seen himself in a B romance movie while running through the airport, he now saw himself an action movie. That thought calmed him for a moment: such situations only happened in the movies. Perhaps Luna was not answering his cell phone simply because... No, no explanation came to him.

On Saturday at four o'clock in the afternoon, he met Emi at the Mito station. He put his backpack in a box at the station to run faster and arrived at the museum in twenty-four minutes. At the gate they paused for a moment to recover from their breathlessness and decide how to proceed.

There were two options: ask for Kiyoshi and confront him or go around the museum looking for clues.

Neither of them felt Sherlock Holmes or, to stay more on

topic, Detective Conan; therefore, they set off toward the main building in search of Kiyoshi.

At the entrance, they asked to speak with the museum director. The young man at the front desk, a young man with glasses and a friendly smile, greeted them courteously and introduced himself as Hiroshi. He wore a smart uniform, perfectly in line with the museum's refined environment.

"Please follow me," Hiroshi said, pointing to the elevator with an elegant gesture. They went up to the second floor (or third, in the Japanese way of counting floors), and as they walked together down a well-lit corridor with polished marble floors and pictures on the walls telling the history of the place, Hiroshi chatted amiably.

"Our director is very passionate about local history," he explained. "He has personally curated many of the exhibits you see here. If you have any specific questions, he will certainly be happy to help you."

"It's a very impressive place," commented Gabriele, feigning interest while his thoughts were at the nearby encounter with Kiyoshi. How would he deal with it? "I had never been there before. I hope I can visit it quietly," he continued in his stunted Japanese.

"Certainly," Hiroshi replied. "We have a new wing devoted to the archaeological discoveries of recent years. The director will be happy to show it to you."

They stopped in front of a finely carved wooden door, which exuded an air of ancient elegance. Hiroshi knocked discreetly. After a few unanswered moments, the boy apologized infinitely, as if the absence of the director was a consequence of his unforgivable failure.

"I'm very sorry, he must be engaged in an unexpected reunion," he said in a trembling voice. "Let me escort you back to the lobby. I can make an appointment for you if you like."

As they retraced their steps, walking quickly but silently, Hiroshi continued to apologize. "The director is usually very punctual," he explained. "Something really urgent must have happened."

"Don't worry," Gabriele reassured him. "It happens to everyone to have unexpected events."

When they reached the entrance, he greeted them with a deep bow, keeping his professional smile. "Thank you for your understanding. It will be a pleasure to arrange a meeting with the director as soon as possible."

They agreed on a new appointment for the day, which they hoped they would not have to resort to, and Hiroshi returned to his seat at the reception desk, visibly relieved.

"In and out like a revolving door," said Emi dejectedly.

Gabriele did not answer; he was absorbed in looking across the large garden that surrounded the main buildings of the museum.

"Okay," said Gabriele thoughtfully. "I am Conan and you are Ayumi. What do we know?"

"Conan I'll do it, you be Kogoro Mori if you want," Emi diluted the tension, referring to the bungling detective Conan works with.

"Luna-chan most likely got here, then went up two flights of stairs," he said.

"Upward or downward?"

"It doesn't say that."

"Kiyoshi's office is on the third floor, counting floors in the Japanese way," observed Gabriele. "So, he could have walked up two flights of stairs to get to the office. But then what? Surely nothing serious could have happened Luna there so we should have also seen the two flights down, four flights in all. What does that mean?"

"That Luna was never in Kiyoshi's office. So, he told the truth?"

"But Luna got here and went up the two flights of stairs, then that was it. Look at the building over there."

"The one across the park?" asked Emi, in a slightly worried tone. "A little creepy..."

"Let's go and see."

They walked through the large park, their shoes sinking into the mud created after the previous day's rain. The plants and bushes, still damp, gave off an earthy, fresh smell. The bare trees cast long shadows on the dark grass, creating a surreal and slightly ominous atmosphere.

Arriving in front of the building, Emi observed the structure. was one story, gray concrete and unadorned. The walls showed signs of deterioration, with cracks snaking along the surface like dark veins. Some windows were boarded up and others covered in dust, obscuring the view inside.

"The door is locked, the building looks empty, maybe it's an old storage room," Emi said, approaching the front door. "Let's see if you can get in through the back."

Gabriele followed her, taking a closer look at the building. Every step they took in the park seemed to echo in that ghostly silence. He noticed that the roof was slightly sloping, covered with moss and fallen leaves. The darkness that now loomed over Ibaraki gave the building a ghostly glow, accentuated by the fog that was beginning to rise from the damp ground.

As they bypassed the building, they found a small back door, half hidden by vines. Emi pushed it slightly but it seemed to be closed as well.

"Let's try to pick the lock," suggested Gabriele, trying to keep calm despite the eerie atmosphere.

Emi nodded, trying to pry it open with a small hook she had in her bag. After a few attempts, the lock gave way with a resounding click. The door slowly opened, revealing a dark and cold interior.

"Little Emi-chan is full of surprises," Gabriele managed to joke.

"As a child, together with Luna-chan, we used to have fun building a variety of things, including locks. So, I know them a little bit, and these are really simple."

They entered cautiously, turning on the flashlights of their phones to illuminate the room. The interior was bare, with old rusty metal shelves and cardboard boxes stacked haphazardly. The concrete floor was covered with debris and cobwebs. Gabriele and Emi advanced slowly, each step raising small clouds of dust.

He had started out in the romantic movie, moved on to action movie, and now found himself in a horror movie. Cold, damp air filled the room, and their breathing was the only sound besides the ticking of water drops seeping through the roof.

"This place is really creepy," whispered Emi, looking around with concern.

"Yes, but we have to find Luna," replied Gabriele, determined not to let fear take over. As soon as they were inside, they shone their cell phone flashlights and saw a staircase leading downward. The hallway was narrow and the walls were covered with mold, giving off a stale smell.

"The two flights of stairs," they said in unison, their voices echoing in the overwhelming silence.

As they descended the stairs, the sound of their footsteps echoed ominously in the darkness. They began to call Luna's name in fearful whispers. Gabriele's heart was beating hard in his chest, every fiber of his being tense and ready to react to whatever might happen.

"Luna? Are you here?" murmured Emi, the tone of her voice full of apprehension.

Getting no response, they began to call louder as their fear gave way to growing worry for their missing friend. Their echo was lost in the meanders of the basement, amplifying the anguish they felt.

"Luna!" cried Gabriele, his voice sounding like a desperate call.

When they reached the bottom of the two flights of stairs, they stopped shouting for a moment and listened carefully. Darkness seemed to envelop them; the silence was almost palpable. It was then that they heard a faint voice, almost a whisper, that seemed to come from a room ahead.

"I am here..."

OMIYA, JAPAN

Monday, January 27, 2019

Luna had been discharged that morning from the hospital. Aside from a little dehydration and a more serious onset of frostbite, she was fine.

At that moment they were in Seizeriya having a quick hamburger and pizza lunch. The television screens in the diner continued to show Commander Komatsu of the Ibaraki Police Department bowing and apologizing for not being able to find Luna sooner and having, he made it clear indirectly, underestimated the danger.

In addition to this, the face of Kiyoshi Sakubu, who had become Japan's number one wanted man, continued to be shown. Poor Hiroshi, the boy at the museum reception desk who had accompanied them and had been so kind to them, had also been interviewed. He said that the last time he had seen Kiyoshi had been only a few minutes before Emi and Gabriele arrived. He had probably left through some emergency exit when he saw them coming and disappeared. The manhunt across the country was at an all-time high.

Luna had been quickly interrogated by the police. She had told them that she had been taken to that building with the explanation that Kiyoshi preferred to stay away from the museum's noise. She now understood that she had been naïve but really had no reason to doubt Kiyoshi.

She had recounted that she did not receive any violence, other than the first assault, and that her abductor gave her little food, water, and a blanket.

When asked by the police about the possible reasons for the aggression and kidnapping, she had replied that she did not understand the reason for it, that Kiyoshi had been delirious about something but that, in his agitation, she did not understand.

She actually remembered it very well but was not yet ready to tell the story to all of Japan. The discovery of the real existence of the Utsuro Bune, and how the red-haired princess was Marianna Paris, would have been communicated in quite another way.

She thought back to those, except Gabriele and Emi who knew everything, who had received information from her about that story.

To her boss, Kato-san, she had only told him about an exciting discovery that would keep her busy for a few days. When he had phoned her to ask how she was doing, he had not wanted to tire her by asking her about the subject and had only told her that she could return to work when she felt up to it.

Gentle Ito-san, Choshi's librarian, could have perhaps guessed what the ultimate object of Luna's research was but could not have connected that research to the event that happened.

"Kiyoshi is a Satake..." repeated Emi to herself, looking at the lemon floating in the Coke. Her voice was lost in the noise of the club but it was clear that she was trying to put the pieces of the puzzle together.

"But are you missing the point?" asked Luna, raising her tone of voice slightly. "The Utsuro Bune is located somewhere in Japan!"

A six or seven-year-old boy, with bob hair and a soft ice cream in his hand, approached curiously. "The Utsuro Bune is a spaceship of extraterrestrials. Does that mean there are extraterrestrials in Japan?" he asked, with an ingenuous smile.

Luna smiled back. "No, don't worry, no extraterrestrials in Japan." Then she turned seriously toward her comrades, "Let's get out of here."

They were on a cold day in late January, the warm sunshine unable to counteract the biting frost in the air. They sat on a wooden bench, slightly damp from morning condensation. The park was almost desert, only a few hurried passersby and crows cawing on the bare branches of the trees.

"Do you really want to go after the boat?" asked Gabriele, hinting at a slight worried smile.

"Of course I do! And don't try to explain to me that I shouldn't, that it can be..." Gabriele put a finger to her lips. "Shhh... Calm down, you just got out of the hospital. I'll help you to find it."

Luna smiled. Only now, after the danger she had escaped, did her heart warm as she saw him near her again and realized how much she had missed him.

"The Satake clan, or what is left of it, has been searching for the vessel for two hundred years. Kiyoshi has given me the impression that he is certain that it is still in Japan. Perhaps he is aware of some interrogation record passed down by word of mouth," Luna said, clasping her gloved hands to warm herself.

"Or it's just a hope, the only one that would remove the disgrace from his clan," Emi replied, trying to blow on his hands to warm up.

"Emi-chan, now don't start being pessimist like Gabriele too," Luna replied. "Kiyoshi, on the other hand, did not give me the impression that he knew the connection with Marianna Paris. The Italian flag was in the folder they filed relatively to the Utsuro Bune but, without the software Gabriele used, the name 'Marianna' was illegible."

"So," Gabriele added, "Kiyoshi had much more information at his disposal than we did but did not know that the Princess was Volta's mistress. Our advantage can only be this."

"Alright," Luna said, squeezing into her coat. "Let's put ourselves in Marianna's shoes. We don't know, and probably never will, why but we do know the who, where, how, and when of the event. This girl arrives in Choshi in a craft that even in our day would be considered advanced. She is in a hostile world but she is definitely helped by the Shoya, otherwise she would have been immediately handed over to higher authorities, regardless of the U.S. search."

Gabriele stood up and, walking back and forth on the icy gravel of the path, continued, "She is welcomed to Choshi but must be hidden and, with her, the boat. Why are you smiling?" he asked surprised, looking at Luna.

"You haven't lost the habit of walking back and forth when you think," she replied, still smiling, as his breath created small clouds of condensation in the cold air.

Gabriele stopped and stared at her, the smile he had missed so much.

"Hey, lovebirds," said Emi after a few seconds of silence. "Shall we continue?"

Gabriele resumed, "If Marianna came to a stranger and dangerous land, it is probably because she had no choice and the boat was no longer usable, so she could not escape to the sea. That means she probably hid toward hinterland. For the boat, however, it's different: it can't have been taken too far, it must be hidden somewhere on the coast."

Luna opened Google Maps on her smartphone, the map centered on Choshi.

"So, what are we looking for?" asked Emi. "Some cave by the sea?"

Luna replied as she scrolled and zoomed the map, "I believe all the caves in the Choshi area were beaten palm to palm during the search for the boat. We are looking for something related to Italy or even Marianna Paris."

"A grove dedicated to her where they may have hidden the boat?" asked Gabriele wryly.

"A grove no," Luna said pointing to a spot on the map, "but maybe a beach yes!" Emi and Gabriele started up. "Choshi Marina Beach! In the report of Shoya's interrogation, two suspects gave hints that could point to that place: one of the suspects mentioned a 'rare woman.' 'Rare' in Japanese is 'Mare' and the suffix for 'Woman' is 'Na'. In practice, the suspect may have said 'Marena', too similar to 'Marina' to be a case. Another suspect then mentioned a hideout to the south, and Choshi Marina Beach is just south of where Marianna is believed to have landed! Also, right next to the beach, is this knoll with vertical walls that may have small coves suitable for hiding something."

"But 'Marina' is a fairly common name for a seaside place, isn't it?" asked Emi, unconvinced.

"Two hundred years ago, it wasn't." Luna replied. "And it's definitely a potential hiding place anyway. Who will accompany me?"

Gabriele was not very convinced but, in fact, there were no

better ways.

"Present," he replied.

"But when are you going back to Italy? Don't you have to work?" she asked.

Luna, a little worried to hear his answer.

"I can work from here. I brought the PC and can continue programming my little car game."

Luna widened her eyes, "You're kidding, right?" "Unfortunately, yes. Don't worry though, I took vacation for all the week," and then he added as he lowered his gaze, "and you are more important."

"There they go again," said Emi, understanding. "But, Luna-chan, isn't it dangerous? Kiyoshi is still around."

"You will protect me," Luna joked, thinking that by now Kiyoshi's purpose of keeping her locked up was no longer significant, since other people also knew her secret.

Emi also agreed to accompany her but knew well that the two of them could not protect her.

Since it took about four hours by train to go from Omiya to Choshi, they decided to leave immediately and stay overnight near Choshi Marina Beach, so they would have plenty of time the next day.

CHOSHI, JAPAN

Tuesday, January 28, 2019

Luna, Emi, and Gabriele arrived at the Choshi Marina Beach on a cold morning in late January. The sun had just risen, painting the sky in shades of pink and orange, but the bitter cold made them huddle in their coats. The beach was completely deserted, which added to the surreal atmosphere. There was no one in sight, no noise except the faint lapping of waves gently crashing on the shore.

The sand was compact and wet, marked only by their footprints, which seemed to be the first in a long time. The vastness of the area, combined with the silence, created a feeling of isolation. The winter sea was calm, the waves moving slowly, reflecting the pale winter sky. "It should be right here," Luna said, looking at the cell phone and then looking up at the horizon.

Looking closely at the coastline, they noticed a small inlet in the rock. They faced a tall, dark rock face with striations that seemed to tell stories of past geological eras. A marked shadow indicated the entrance to a hidden cave.

"Look there." She pointed to Gabriele, with a gesture of her chin. They approached cautiously, their hearts beating little faster with excitement and uncertainty. The sand became rougher as they approached the rock. The small cove was partially concealed by creepers and dried seaweed attached to the rock walls.

"It's right here," Luna said, her voice betraying a mixture of disbelief and anticipation. "I can't believe we got here."

Gabriele advanced first, lifting a hand to touch the cold surface of the rock. "It's bigger it looked," he said, looking inside the dark opening.

"Very good, however, now let me do it." An ominous voice rang out behind them, chilling the blood in their veins.

They turned and were shocked to see Kiyoshi, with an evil grin on face, pointing a gun at them. His cold, calculating expression made the situation even more frightening.

"Don't say a word. Turn around and enter the cave. I am behind you," he ordered in an icy tone.

Without a choice, they had to obey Kiyoshi's order. The sound of their footsteps was accompanied by the echo of their fear, every noise amplified in the darkness.

The first to advance was Luna, whose courage was fueled by a desire to be the first person to see the Utsuro Bune after more than two hundred years. Emi and Gabriele were immediately behind her while Kiyoshi, two meters away, guarded them with the gun tightly gripped in his hand. The cold metal of the gun glowed in the dim light of the flashlights on their phones, a constant reminder of the threat looming.

The cave was about three meters in diameter. As she walked, Luna could not stop thinking that, according to Kyokutei Bakin's descriptions of the vessel, it was too small for the ship to fit through, but it might have been disassembled to be better hidden. Fear clutched her stomach but she could not stop now. After about ten meters in a straight line, the cave bent ninety degrees to the right. Each step echoed like a drum in the silence, Luna's heart was beating wildly Both danger and the anticipation of discovery.

Three more steps and she would have been able to see what was around the corner.

Two.

One.

She looked with her heart pounding in her chest and, after seeing, almost stopped.

After another two yards, the cave ended. There was nothing there; they had been mistaken. The damp walls of the cave were smooth, with no sign of a hiding place or secret passage. Disappointment and panic mingled, creating a feeling of emptiness.

"What's going on?!" shouted Kiyoshi, with an anger that made the cave walls shake. The sound of his voice booming, amplifying the tension.

At that moment, they heard a loud thump behind them and, an instant later, a thud. They turned sharply and saw Kiyoshi on the ground, unconscious. Behind him, Commandant Komatsu held his gun aloft, gripping it by the barrel. His face was serious but his eyes betrayed relief.

"Are you all right?" asked Komatsu, lowering his weapon and looking at them with concern. The icy air of the cave now seemed a little less oppressive, but the relief was only partial.

"Komatsu-san!" exclaimed Luna, her voice a mixture of gratitude and confusion. "What are you doing here?"

"I followed you. Emi-san warned me about your movements because she was worried, and she did well," replied Komatsu in a calm but firm tone.

Luna and Gabriele turned to Emi, their eyes full of gratitude. "Emi-chan, you saved us," Luna said, hugging her sister with a warmth that conveyed all her affection and relief.

Komatsu, meanwhile, bent over Kiyoshi, who lay unconscious on the ground. With an expert movement, the commander bound his wrists with handcuffs. "Are you all right?" he asked again, as his gaze passed carefully over each of them to make sure they were indeed safe.

"Yes," Emi and Gabriele replied in unison, still shaken but relieved.

"Not much," Luna said instead with a thoughtful sigh. "This was perhaps our last hope of finding the Utsuro Bune."

Komatsu paused, his face betraying his surprise. "To find what?" he asked, evidently stupefied. His gaze was full of curiosity as his eyes scanned Luna for an explanation.

"It's a long story," Emi replied, looking at him with a tired smile.

TOKYO, JAPAN

Thursday, January 30, 2019

Luna and Gabriele strolled through Yoyogi Park, remembering when they had been there with their friends a few years earlier.
"Marco and Hiah are still engaged, right?" asked Gabriele.
"Yes, they now live together in a small apartment near Midtown. Hiah got a job in the Japanese headquarters of LG," Luna replied, smiling at the thought of their friends.
"Ah good, so they have settled down! Marco wrote to me in October saying they changed his contract. He is now an employee of the Japanese office and no longer an expatriate. The salary is lower but now he can make plans for the future." He looked at Luna and added, with a hint of wistfulness, "Lucky him."
Luna looked at him with a slightly sad smile. "Shall we stop for coffee?"
They took a seat in a café just outside the park. Despite the high price of nearly five dollars for an espresso, the quality was Italian, and Gabriele enjoyed every sip.
"You still haven't said anything to your boss about the Utsuro Bune?" asked Gabriele, breaking the silence.
"No, I'll go to the library on Monday and tell him about it in person," Luna replied, turning the teaspoon back into the cup.
"It was an outstanding discovery, you're going to be famous!" exclaimed Gabriele, trying to instill enthusiasm.
"I guess so," Luna replied with a half-smile. It was clear that she was disappointed that she had not come full circle by finding the boat.
On the screens on the walls could be seen, as just a few days earlier, Commander Komatsu and Kiyoshi, but this time the roles were reversed: Komatsu was receiving a medal and Kiyoshi, handcuffed, was being loaded into police car. He was shouting nonsense phrases about how his clan had been falsely accused, that the boat did not exist, and that, therefore, it was not their

fault that it had not been found.

No one but the two of them and Emi understood what he was talking about.

"I'm happy for Komatsu," Gabriele said, watching the television. Receiving no response from Luna, he turned his gaze her and saw her absorbed in looking at her cell phone.

"You are a poor company," he told her jokingly.

Luna resurfaced from her thoughts and replied, "The more I think about it, the more it seems to me that Choshi Marina Bay was the perfect place for the search. I was reviewing the record of the interrogation at Shoya on my cell phone and, aside from the one who said he wanted to return to the cave, the other two suspects had given clues in that direction."

Gabriele stared at her in silence.

"Evidently 'Marena' did not stand for 'Marina' but for 'Marianna,' he had simply repeated the woman's name hoping, with that information, to save his own life but the samurai questioning him did not understand what he was saying. The second, on the other hand, may have given the wrong clue to help Marianna in her escape. Must have really been a special woman to have made a whole country want to protect her," Luna continued.

Gabriele had not changed his expression; he stared at her intensively.

"Poor things, who knows how delirious they were, under torture and close to the death... Gabriele! Will you stop looking at me like that?"

"What is it that he said?" asked Gabriele in a grave voice, a mixture of surprise and irritation. "Why didn't you ever tell me about the first suspect?"

"What did who say? I didn't tell you about them because they don't mean anything, not even for the Satake clan, which hasn't done anything with them for two hundred years. And what is this tone?" replied Luna, confused and a little irritated.

Gabriele raised his voice, so much so that everyone in the club turned to look at him. "They didn't make anything of it because they are Japanese and can read kanji! I don't!" then he continued, in a lower but still extremely excited tone of voice. "We thought our only advantage over the Satake was that we knew the identity of the woman in the Utsuro Bune, actually we had another advantage: I don't know kanji, so I don't let it affect me, you and the Satake clan do. How is 'return to the cave' written?"

Luna did not understand but showed him the line: 洞窟へ帰る.

"Here: the first two kanji mean 'cave,' the last two mean 'return'."

"Exactly!" said Gabriele. "A Japanese sees the kanji and reads 'return,' without any hesitation, without any doubt, but the suspect was talking, screaming, delirious! The person said 'dōkutsu kaeru'!"

Luna did not understand. She said in a low voice, "Exactly, 'dōkutsu kaeru' means 'return to the cave.'"

"Or?" asked Gabriele with a complicit smile.

Luna did not understand, so he continued, "Imagine the scene: samurai tortures a poor peasant, he is about to die, to save himself he manages to say two words: dōkutsu and kaeru. Think of them said verbally, not written in kanji."

Luna's gaze went from incomprehension, to suspicion, to disbelief, to joy. She sprang to her feet and shouted, "'Kaeru' did not mean 'return'! It meant 'Frog'!" Now the whole café stared at her.

"That's right," said Gabriele. "The person did not say 'cave-return', as misinterpreted by the Samurai and written in the report, but 'cave-frog'. The Utsuro Bune is hidden under Mount Tsukuba."

ANTONIO MORI

TOKYO, JAPAN

Friday, June 9, 2023

'CEO'.

Gabriele turned the newly printed business card over in his hands, looking at the three-letter abbreviation listed under his name.

Above his, was that of the company: 'Parisolo Co.Ltd.'

He was in his office on the 32nd floor of Toranomon hills in downtown Tokyo.

Despite the role, he felt a child's excitement at having that new toy, so he got up and headed to the next office to find Luna to show her. As he came out of his office, he saw that the nameplate for the one across the street had also arrived, which read 'Emi Kobayashi, R&D Director.' He knocked on the door next to his, the one bearing the nameplate 'Luna Kobayashi, President.'

No one answered. He knocked again, then remembered: that Friday a fifth grader from Chiba was visiting their offices.

The story of their company was wildly famous, and schools would line up to hear the stories of Marianna Paris from Luna Kobayashi herself.

He then headed to the room dedicated to the museum; thirty square meters that cost a fortune, did not yield a yen, but which they would not give up for anything in the world.

The boat had become the centerpiece of the Ibaraki Museum, now with a new director since the old one would be in prison for many years, but other objects were kept in their museum and they would not part with them for any reason.

He opened the door and saw Luna showing Marianna's diary, safely inside a glass case, to a group of about twenty-five boys and girls. Eventually, Luna had partly achieved her dream of becoming a teacher.

He could not contain excitement in thinking about how beautiful she was. Even more so since she was beginning to show the first potbelly that, in a few weeks, would become obvious to everyone.

Luna had reached the point where she recounted that, he had guessed that the Utsuro Bune was located in the caves of Mt. Tsukuba, it had been fairly easy to discover the exact location by following upstream the only watercourse that, starting right from Choshi came to Lake Sotonakasaura and then entered Lake Kasumigaura, which he and Luna had visited before arriving at Mount Tsukuba during the trip that, five years earlier, had ended the first part of their relationship and which had allowed him to connect the words 'cave' and 'frog'.

North of the lake, one then had to take the Koise kawa and, finally, the Kawamata kawa, which had its source right in a cave on Mount Tsukuba.

Luna continued the story to the children by explaining that in that cave, hidden by thick vegetation and thus from view from the outside, they had found the mythical craft. Gabriele thought that it had not been as easy as she was telling it: he had almost broken his arm while walking through the cave, trying to move a rock that hid the last passage to the craft, and Emi had made a five-feet flight, fortunately without consequences, exploring some burrows; however, it was not necessary to report those details to the children.

She then recounted the excitement the three had felt when their flashlights had lit up the Peach, with so much of name written on the hull, like any self-respecting boat (the famous 'enigmatic scriptures' mentioned by Kyokutei Bakin that had fascinated scholars of this mystery for two centuries).

They had managed to open the Peach and, inside a closed box, found the most precious treasure of all: Marianna's diary.

She recounted in detail her affair, first a love affair and then a scientific, with Alessandro Volta; her voyage between the Atlantic and the Pacific, complete with naval battles with French brigands off the coast of Argentina; finally, she wrote of her chance arrival in Japan when, by now exhausted, she had decided to break off her journey at the first place she had arrived. She recounted how the chief of the village where she had arrived had welcomed her with friendship and helped her hide her embarkation. He had given her provisions and suggested that she escaped as far north as possible, where he evidently thought it would be safer for her, asking in return only for that piece of cloth colored green, white, and red, having probably been convinced that it was a magic cloth and it was because of the formulas written on that cloth that the boat could move without sails or oars.

She ended by writing about how she had decided to leave the journal with the Peach so that her discoveries would not be completely lost.

Within the journal, Luna, Gabriele, and Emi had found the formula for an alcohol compound that Marianna had named Elixir. They had managed to reproduce it thanks Emi's technical skills and realized that it almost tripled the efficiency of the best combustion cells currently available, if designed with a semi-spherical shape as for the system used in the Peach.

Less consumption, virtually no pollution, and cheap energy available everywhere. A dream comes true.

They had told the world about the discovery and decided not to patent it, as it was not theirs but Marianna's. They had only demanded that the new alcohol be called Parisolo, after the surname of its discoverer.

For the same reason they had also decided to name their company after that, the first to specialize in the production of this alcohol and its marketing.

Success had been immediate, and Gabriele had finally had the chance to move to Japan and live together with Luna.

He continued to observe her speaking to the children with affection; he was moved by imagining seeing her speak to their son.

He saw a very sweet little girl raising her hand and asking a question that he could not understand.

Instead, he understood that Luna had replied that they could not find that out and, probably, no one would ever know.

When the presentation was over, Luna greeted the class and saw

Gabriele in the doorway staring at her.

She smiled and approached him.

"Look," said Gabriele proudly and smiling. "My business cards just arrived; they say CEO."

Luna smiled understandingly. "You are so baka." Then she added thoughtfully, "Did you see how cute that little girl was? She had such a thoughtful and intelligent look."

"The one who asked you last question? What did he ask you?"

"Yes, she. She asked me if you know where Marianna went or what happened to her then," Luna replied. "She has very big eyes and a peculiar hair color, she must have parents with Western ancestry. I wonder if our child will also have such beautiful eyes."

Gabriele hugged Luna, "If takes after her mother, they will surely be beautiful."

They remained hugging each other, watching the group move away from the museum, especially that sweet, intelligent little girl with big eyes and fiery red hair.

AUTHOR'S NOTE

Like any self-respecting writer of historical novels, I too feel compelled to explain which of the facts in this book are true or, at least, documented.

Let's start with the main character: Marianna Paris is a real-life person, and her romantic relationship with Alessandro Volta is documented. Marianna is described as a talented actress with beautiful red hair. Equally true is that it was the Emperor Austria himself who bothered to put an end to the relationship that was considered embarrassing for such an important cultural figure in the kingdom. After Volta's marriage, there is no longer any documentation about Marianna.

Volta's relations with Galvani and Lavoisier are historically documented, as are all the technical explanations that Emi offers Luna in front of the oyakudon in their home.

The arrival of a spherical craft in Japan in 1803 is reported in several sources, including Kyokutei Bakin's book Toen Shōsetsu, published in 1825 and cited in the preface. This event gave rise to numerous theories, including that of a possible encounter with an extraterrestrial civilization. The references to Japanese language, particularly writing, are also accurate. For example, the term 'kaeru' can mean both "return" and "frog," although it is written with different kanji.

The use of a secret code based on radicals, such as the one Luna discovered at the Enpuku-Ji temple, is documented.

Finally, Mount Tsukuba actually exists, and it is truly called "frog mountain" because of the presence of many statues of this amphibian, which are considered good luck.

Made in the USA
Middletown, DE
28 February 2025

On February 22, 1803, a strange boat landed on the east coast of Japan: it was spherical in shape, the top was bright red, and the bottom was made of metal. Even more bizarre is its sole occupant: a foreign woman with flowing red hair. At that time, however, Japan, under the Tokugawa hegemony, was a closed country: the woman was soon turned away, and the story of her arrival was lost in time until it became legend.

Bergamo, 2019. It is an ordinary Saturday afternoon and Gabriele is working on the development of a video game: he is employed in a large multinational company in the automotive field, but his free time is dedicated to other projects. Just as he is trying to regain his concentration, a message comes to him: it is Luna, the woman he loved in the three years he was in Japan, and whom he may never have stopped loving. He does not even have a chance to lose himself in memories, that Luna asks him for help in solving a riddle she came across during her research for her thesis: in the Ibaraki museum, among 18th-century documents, she found an Italian flag. "Impossible," Luna immediately thinks; "impossible" is what Gabriele says.

In front of them lies a two-century-old mystery, immersed in Napoleonic battles, political intrigue and extraordinary scientific discoveries; a story that winds between Italy and Japan, on whose trail, however, they are not the only ones.

ISBN 9798335079242

9 798335 079242

90000

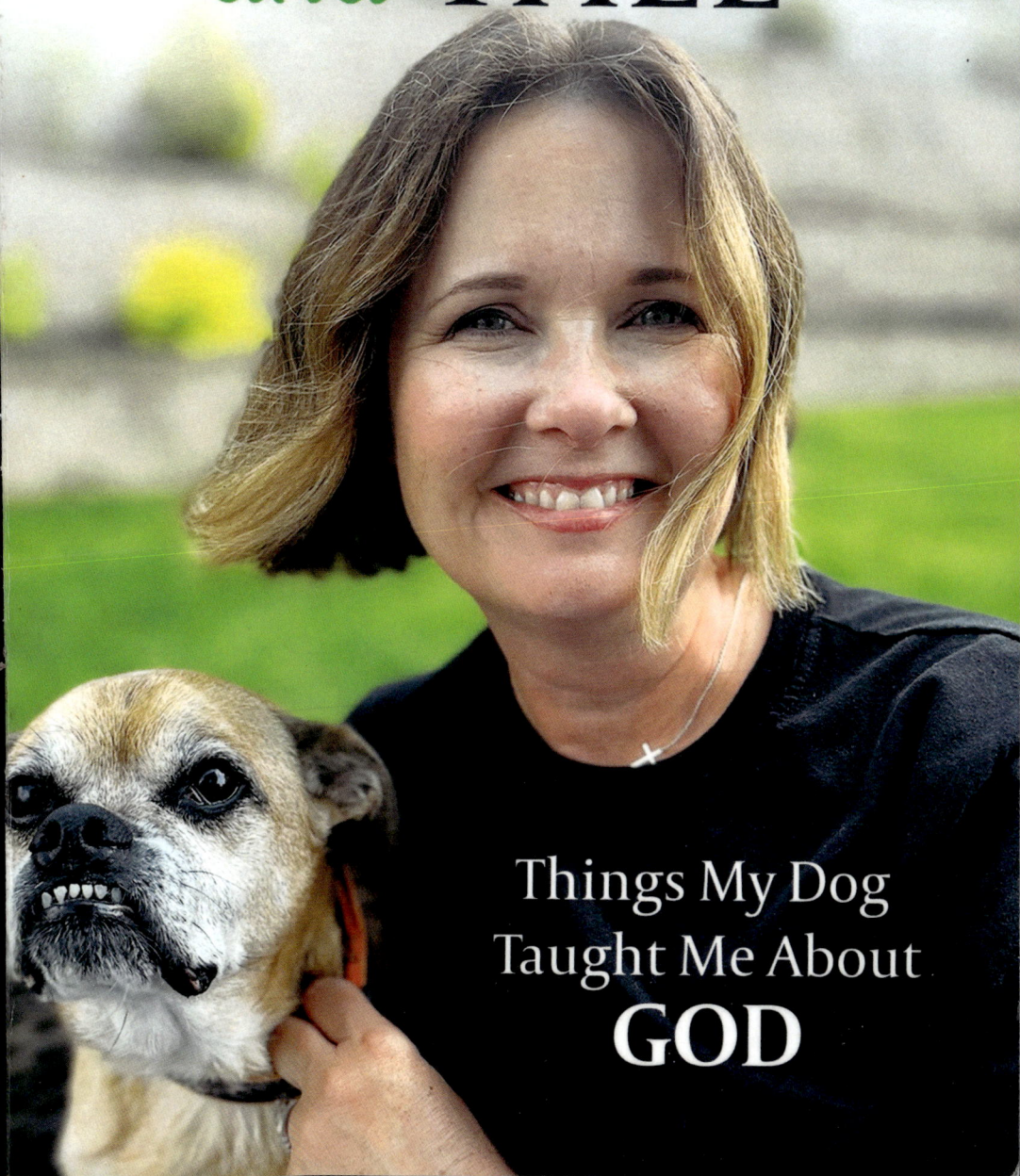

LISA WEIGARD
CHARLIE, ME, and THEE

Things My Dog
Taught Me About
GOD